"He's not a murderer!" Ari proclaimed, suddenly stopping and facing Molly. "He didn't do it," Ari emphasized. "Molly, I've known Bob for most of my life. We have a very special relationship, and I believe in his innocence."

Ari's passion touched Molly. She placed her hands gently on Ari's shoulders before she spoke. "Then let me do my job."

"I will. But I can't see Bob go to jail for something he didn't do."

"Do you know where he is, Ari?" Molly asked, her eyes probing Ari's for the truth.

"No," Ari answered honestly.

"But if you did, would you tell me?" Ari hesitated and Molly shook her head. "Then I have to think I can't trust you."

"I'm sorry. But you don't get it."

Molly threw up her hands and sighed. They stared at each other, unable to resolve their differences. "I guess there's nothing else to say," Molly concluded. She turned to walk away.

"Molly, wait," Ari said. Molly faced her and she could see Ari was searching for words and tears were coming down her face. Finally she asked, "Have you ever owed a debt you never thought you could repay?"

Visit

Bella Books

at

BellaBooks.com

or call our toll-free number

1-800-729-4992

Paid in Full

Ann Roberts

Bella
BOOKS

2006

Bella Books, Inc.
P.O. Box 10543
Tallahassee, FL 32302

Printed in the United States of America on acid-free paper
First Edition

Editor: Anna Chinappi
Cover designer: Stephanie Solomon-Lopez

ISBN 1-59493-059-7

This book is dedicated to my mother,
the first writer I ever knew.

Acknowledgments

I am grateful to many people for their help with this endeavor—

Linda Hill for the opportunity

All the folks at Bella Books who keep the fires of the independent press burning

Anna Chinappi for her insight and guidance

LC who explained the details of police work

KS for pushing me to finish

My family—the ones who had to wait until I got off the computer. I'm fortunate to be so loved.

About the Author

Ann Roberts wrote her first novel at the age of four. *Petunia's Adventure* detailed the odyssey of her pet guinea pig on the day it escaped. Instead of worrying, Ann wrote about her loss and received two important rewards for her efforts: Her guinea pig did reappear and her mother baked her cookies because she thought the story was wonderful.

Ann has worked as an educator for twenty years in the high school and community college settings. She also spent thirty-five minutes in a kindergarten class, an experience she still cannot discuss. Currently she is a middle school administrator and lives with her family in Phoenix.

Chapter One
Sunday, June 17
4:20 p.m.

When Ari opened the door, the last thing she expected to see was a corpse, but there he was, face down, spread eagle on the floor, sunlight washing over his lifeless body. She reflexively gasped and backed out of the house. A few seconds passed, and when no one jumped out and attacked her, she took a breath and re-entered. Her footfalls echoed against the bare walls, the house vacated months ago by retirees spending their golden years in Florida. She advanced to the body and froze, listening to her heart pounding and the distant hum of lawnmowers.

Ari studied the victim with emotional detachment, a skill she'd learned at the police academy. Male. Probably mid-forties, salt and pepper hair, soft hands, the fingertips of the right one drenched in blood. His gold Rolex, expensive Italian loafers and pin-striped suit attested to his wealth. Judging from the condition of the body, Ari doubted he'd been dead for long. A puddle of blood surrounded his middle, suggesting an abdominal wound.

She winced at the sight of the floor. Her clients had spent the past two months renovating the house, which included refinishing the original hardwood. She scanned the ancient plaster walls adjusting to their recent coat of paint, and her eyes drifted to the vaulted ceilings and the refurbished crown molding. A historic home, every square foot had been given a total makeover to justify the high asking price for the small amount of space.

The only thing out of place was the bar that the owner had insisted on installing in the living room. It ruined the aesthetics in Ari's opinion, and she avoided looking at its black countertop and chrome fixtures. With ten steps, Ari stood under the archway that led to the tiny galley kitchen. The white cabinets and ceramic tile were almost too bright against the morning sunlight, but nothing was disturbed, and there wasn't a speck of blood anywhere.

She shook her head and returned to the living room. It took a lot to surprise her, and she'd seen most everything in twelve years of real estate, but this was a new one. Unable to stand still, but hesitant to leave, she checked her watch. The young couple who were viewing the property wouldn't arrive for another twenty minutes. Ari knew she should go back outside to her SUV and call the police. She should not snoop, but curiosity won over, and she found herself looking down the short hallway. Although the doors were open, little light emitted from the adjacent rooms, and a tingle crept up Ari's back.

It was definitely spooky. She veered into the only bathroom and stared at the shower door. There were no shadows silhouetted against the antique frosted glass, but she felt her breath catch as she swung the door open, revealing only sparkling blue ceramic tiles. Ari crossed into the small bedroom, where eggshell-white walls and contrasting wallpaper trim greeted her. The closet door stood ajar, just as she had left it after her last showing. She remembered the client had tried to close it out of habit, but Ari had quickly pulled it open again. A closed door was a sign that sellers had something to hide.

A chainsaw roared suddenly and Ari jumped. She realized it was too clear and too close.

She carefully made her way to the master bedroom and with each step the chainsaw buzz grew louder. The sliding glass door leading to the backyard stood wide open, the sheer curtains fluttering in the slight breeze. Ari realized the noise was coming from a neighboring yard, and she wasn't going to be the victim of a maniac wielding a power tool.

The air conditioner was losing the battle against the 105-degree heat, and the room was baking. Ari saw that someone had pried the door open with a crowbar, breaking the mechanism in half. She nearly shoved it closed to vent her anger but stopped just as her fingers touched the handle. *Damn*. Now she had disturbed a crime scene. A wave of guilt swept over her momentarily, but as the real estate agent, she knew her fingerprints would be everywhere so the damage was minimal.

This was probably the killer's entrance. That realization propelled her back down the hall to the living room. Ari glanced at the front door, her escape route if necessary. She vowed to remain for only another minute. Crouching over the man, she repressed the urge to fish his wallet out of his back pocket, but she wanted further clues to his identity. Her eyes settled on the floor and a few small droplets of blood that trailed behind the bar ten feet away. She swallowed hard and stood up. Walking so as not to disturb any of the blood, Ari peered around the bar. In a split second she realized nothing was wrong and everything was wrong. The shelves were clean and the floor refinishers had actually been able to replace the old wooden planks, worn and water damaged probably from the liquids that would spill off the counter. The bar was untouched, but a bloody stain covered the freshly painted wall behind it. Perhaps this is where he died, Ari thought. He was standing behind the bar, and he fell back against the wall. She moved closer, allowing her eyes to adjust to the dark space behind the bar. At first she thought it was only a blood spatter, the sunlight not illuminating the niche at all. Then she realized it was a word, a name. *"Robert"* was crudely scrawled right above the baseboard. The color on the wall matched the color on the floor, and her mind flashed to the victim's blood-caked fingertips.

A strange sound broke the silence.

Ari couldn't tell if it came from inside or outside, but her curiosity instantly vanished. She bolted upright, smashing her head against the shelves that used to hold beer steins from around the world. She cursed fiercely as she scurried past the dead man and slammed the front door. Maybe that would scare the intruder away, if someone really was there.

She sprinted to the SUV, looking left and right. Only after she'd locked herself inside the truck and pulled her revolver from the glove box did she feel safe. She must have been quite a sight. Cell phone in one hand, gun in the other. She whirled around, checking the back, but no one was there. Now seemed like a good time to call the police.

Ari made the necessary 911 call and then immediately punched in her buyer's number to cancel the showing. An answering machine picked up, and she knew they were probably on their way. Usually real estate wasn't this exciting, but there had been a few interesting moments, such as when she had caught a couple having sex in the hot tub of one of her vacant listings. She cracked a smile at the memory of their horrified expressions. What really stood out in her mind was the beautiful woman emerging from the steam, her breasts glistening.

She took a deep breath, her heart still galloping and her hands shaking. She returned the gun to the glove compartment, chastising herself for not retrieving it *before* she searched the house. Her head started to pound and she rubbed her temples. She'd forgotten what it was like to experience an adrenaline rush.

The SUV suddenly felt like a sauna. Even dogs weren't supposed to be kept in enclosed vehicles during Phoenix summers. Rummaging through the center console, Ari found a clip in the compartment and pulled her long, black hair into a makeshift bun, noting one reason why most lesbians have short haircuts. She checked once more through all the windows before she opened the door and slid out, throwing her jacket on the seat as an offering to the June sun. She desperately craved a cold beer and a swimming pool, preferably in the company of a beautiful woman. If she couldn't have that, she would have gladly settled for a pair of shorts and sandals. Anything to shed the Italian loafers that were pasted to her feet. The worst part of real estate was definitely the power dressing. If she could sell houses from her couch clad in sweats and a T-shirt, she would have been thrilled.

Ari strolled around the truck, stretching out her long legs and forgetting that she was a target under the sun's magnifying glass. She surveyed the nearby homes, every yard immaculate and every house possessing curbside appeal. The neighborhood was alive on this Sunday afternoon, complete with chirping birds and pounding hammers that joined the ever present roar of the lawnmowers. Ari began to doubt that the sound she'd heard inside was sinister. More than likely it was a neighbor working in his yard. Until today, she would have believed this area was virtually immune to the high Phoenix crime rate.

Down the road the black-and-white units approached, three of them. The coroner's wagon and detectives couldn't be far behind. Ari smiled when the first officer emerged from his patrol car. Ben Hastings had been a family friend for years. He had watched Ari grow up, and like many of the officers, he still saw her as "Big Jack Adams's little girl" and perpetually sixteen years old. He lumbered up the sidewalk, his husky frame testing the seams of his uniform.

"Ari Adams, what are you doing here?" Ben asked, as he pecked her on the cheek.

"I found the victim," she said.

Ben noticed the real estate sign in the yard with Ari's name in big, bold letters and nodded. A sly smile crept over his face. "You didn't disturb the crime scene, did you, Ari? You know, poke around or anything?"

"As a matter of fact, I heard a noise after I discovered him, so I got out of there fast." He didn't notice that she had avoided his question, but his expression sobered at the thought of an intruder.

"We'll check it out." He motioned for the officers, and the group fanned out around the property.

The other crime scene vehicles arrived and Ari watched the circus unfold. As a witness, she knew she couldn't leave. Just as she opened her cell phone to try the buyers again, a white Maxima pulled up to the curb.

"Shit," she mumbled, meandering through the throng of people and vehicles, thinking of what excuse she could give to the bewildered buyers.

"Excuse me," someone said behind her. Ari turned and locked eyes with a woman who matched her five-eleven frame, but could have wrestled her to the ground in a second. Most of her bulk was pure muscle, but Ari could see she also carried some extra weight that added to her shapeliness. The woman's short, blond hair curled lightly over high cheekbones and a finely chiseled face. Designer shades masked her eyes. "You're Ari Adams?" she inquired. "I'm Detective Nelson. I need a statement."

Ari nodded and held up a finger indicating she only would be a second as she started toward the buyers' car. Detective Nelson firmly planted a hand on her elbow, stopping her stride. "Ms. Adams, where are you going? I need that statement now."

Ari turned slowly and stared at her reflection through the woman's sunglasses. The detective's impatience was evident and deep creases lined her forehead. "I'm not going anywhere, Detective, but I need to let those people know they won't be viewing this property today." She motioned to the couple, who were now chatting with a neighbor and undoubtedly learning all about the commotion. "Besides," she added, "I'm sure you don't want extra people traipsing around your crime scene."

Molly Nelson nodded, but she wasn't paying attention. The sight of this woman had taken her breath away. She'd just fallen on the murder case of the year, but she found herself lost in Ari Adams's dark green eyes.

"Detective, you need to let me go," Ari said with a broad grin.

Molly glanced down and blushed. Her hand still held Ari's elbow. She quickly withdrew it and murmured, "Sorry," before walking away.

By the time Ari reached the buyers, they were already piling back into the Maxima, sure that the neighborhood was unsafe. She apologized, but as the car sped away, she was certain a commission had too.

She needed aspirin. The yard was flooded with people and equipment, all for the benefit of someone who no longer existed. Cops searched, techs measured, the coroner studied, but nothing could change the outcome. She cocooned herself in the SUV and gulped three aspirin. She watched the blond detective emerge from the house with the coroner, talking on her cell phone while giving instructions to Ben Hastings. It was clear to Ari that whoever was on the other end of that phone made the detective nervous. She nodded constantly, shifted her weight from foot to foot and ran her hand through her hair incessantly. The conversation ended abruptly with the detective pulling the phone from her ear and snapping it shut with one hand. She stared at the phone, and Ari watched her heave her shoulders with a huge sigh as she dropped the phone into her pocket. Ari was fascinated. Detective

Nelson clearly had full command of the investigation, but there was something tentative about her, something unsure. When the detective looked in Ari's direction, their eyes locked and oddly, Ari felt a tingle shoot down her back. Where in the world did that come from?

Detective Nelson frowned, obviously not feeling the same surge of electricity, and marched over to the SUV. "Is now a good time?" she snapped.

Ari's gaze followed the curves of Detective Nelson's body. She was in her mid-thirties, very well endowed and an extra blouse button had come undone, revealing more cleavage than she probably intended. The pale, white ridges rose and fell with her breathing. "Your button," Ari whispered, with a slight motion.

The detective quickly adjusted herself, turning red in the process. "Thanks," she mumbled. She sighed and stuck out her hand in truce. "Maybe we could start over. I'm Detective Molly Nelson."

"Ari Adams." The detective had removed her shades revealing crystal blue eyes that would have been beautiful were it not for the deep bags sagging underneath them. "You look like you could use some of these," Ari offered, holding up the bottle of aspirin.

Molly gratefully swallowed the pills dry. The minute she'd pulled the vic's wallet from his pocket and read his name, she knew her life had immediately changed. This case would make or break her career.

Molly focused on her notepad as her hormones rapidly trampled over her professionalism. Just touching Ari's cool hand made Molly hot, and when Ari spoke, her voice had a breathy, seductive quality, whether Ari meant it to or not.

Ari Adams could have been a model instead of a real estate agent. She oozed grace, even in the way she sat in the leather seat, her long legs crossed and her hands folded in her lap. She formed her smile with perfect lips—legs and lips, the two features Molly always seemed to notice when she looked at a woman. She cleared her throat. "Miss Adams, could you tell me how you found the body?"

Ari retold the story, eliminating the part about her momentary snooping. Molly scribbled, continually nodding throughout the account but watching Ari carefully. Every move Ari made was deliberate. When a strand of her jet black hair fell from the makeshift bun, Ari slowly tucked it back behind her ear with her index finger, a gesture Molly found hypnotic. She tried to focus on Ari's statement, but she couldn't stop staring at the real estate agent. She already knew who Ari was—the daughter of a cop legend. It was hard to believe that the beauty in front of her was related to the bear of a man everyone knew as Big Jack.

"Who else has access to the house?" Molly asked automatically, hoping that she hadn't already asked the question.

"Well, I have a key, there's a key in the lockbox for other agents and service people, and I really couldn't tell you how many other keys my clients have." Molly underlined something in her notebook several times.

"So, tell me about the owners," she said, flipping back a few pages in her notes. "A Mr. and Mrs. Theodore Watson?"

"Well, they're very nice. The Watsons are an elderly couple who have already moved to Florida to retire. I'm really working for their son who has been given power of attorney."

"The son," Molly murmured. "What's his name?"

It was like lightning striking Ari's brain. Molly peered over her notes, conscious of Ari's hesitation. "His name's Bob. Bob Watson."

Molly's head jerked up. "Robert."

Ari tried to hide the emotional torment that was welling inside. The idea of Bob Watson being implicated in a murder was absurd. He was an established member of the community, a business entrepreneur and one of her dearest friends from high school. They had briefly dated before she acknowledged the truth about herself. More importantly, Bob stood by her five years later after she'd been disowned by her parents for choosing an "unnatural lifestyle."

"Ms. Adams, is something wrong?" The detective's voice drew Ari away from the unpleasant memories.

"I'm sorry," she said. The pounding in her head was getting worse. "It's just I know Bob Watson, and there's no way he could be involved in something like this."

The detective flashed a sad smile. She heard this line all the time.

"Look," Ari continued emphatically, "I'm telling you that the message behind the bar is deceptive. It's not . . ."

Her words trailed off as Detective Nelson's expression darkened. "And how would you know about that?"

Ari blushed. "Okay, you caught me. I followed the blood and saw the name on the wall." Molly waited, knowing there was more. Ari wanted to lie, but for some reason, she found she couldn't. "I did look through the other rooms, just to see how much damage there was."

"And?" Molly prompted.

Ari shifted uncomfortably. "I accidentally touched the handle on the patio door." Molly cursed under her breath, sending Ari into a shotgun explanation. "It was dumb, I know better than that, but I can guarantee you my fingerprints will be all over that house anyway."

"And possibly over the fingerprints of the killer," Molly interjected. Ari slumped in the seat, her poise abandoned for the moment. Molly watched Ari massage her temples, her cheeks crimson from embarrassment. An apology tried to work its way from Molly's lips but she swallowed it down. She didn't have anything to be sorry for. Ari deserved to be chewed out, and if it hurt her beautiful feelings, then so be it. Still, Molly found herself planted to the ground, unable to storm away as she was accustomed. She reached over and touched her arm. "You know, Ms.

Adams, for a cop's daughter, you did something pretty foolish," she observed in a kind voice.

The change in demeanor drew Ari's gaze back to Molly's. Ari studied the piercing blue eyes, stern but caring. She stared at Molly a little longer than was polite before smiling. "I don't know what came over me," she said. "Natural curiosity."

"Curiosity killed the cat," Molly countered, as she involuntarily smiled back at Ari. Someone called her name and the smile faded. She nodded to Ari and turned away, mortified by her own behavior. What was she doing, flirting with a civilian at a crime scene? Where was her professionalism? "Focus now, Nelson," she whispered to herself.

Ari watched Molly stride away, the smell of musk still lingering in the truck. To clear her head, Ari hopped out and ventured a few feet onto the grass.

Ben Hastings rounded the corner and called, "You still here?" Ari grinned conspiratorially. She loved joking with Ben. He was a second father to her and the only person who understood why she had left the Tucson Police Department after one short year.

Ben fished a handkerchief from his pants pocket and wiped the sweat from his leathery face. "So did you talk to Nelson?"

"Uh-huh. She took my statement and scolded me for snooping."

Ben wagged a knowing finger and shook his head. He knew Ari would never change. He also noticed her blush when he mentioned Molly Nelson. She was staring at the grass, using the toe of an expensive loafer to pock the ground and avoid his eyes. Ben watched her struggle with her feelings. He loved Ari dearly. She had endured more in her thirty-two years than most people did in an entire lifetime. Everyone had abandoned her in one way or another, but he would always be there. And if anyone deserved an opportunity to find happiness, it was Ari. "Yes," he said plainly.

"What?" Ari asked, only slightly puzzled.

"Yes, she's your type. She's thirty-five, born and raised here, moved away for a while, really good at her job. That's about all I know."

Ari's cheeks flushed. Why did she care? She was in absolutely no position to want any woman. Her career was her life, at least that's what her last lover had believed. She stared down at the large divot and pushed dirt back in the hole. "So who was the guy inside?"

Ben sighed. "You're gonna get me into a lot of trouble, Ari."

"C'mon, Ben," she said, using her voice from childhood, the voice that had always won Ben over, whether it was for another game of checkers or another push on the swing.

Ben scowled and looked around. "Michael Thorndike."

It took only a second for the name to register. "The guy who renovated most of the downtown area? The leader of the Phoenix League?"

"Shhhh." Ben cautioned. "Yes, that Michael Thorndike."

"So how did he die?"

"Two shots from a thirty-eight caliber. One to the chest and one to the gut."

"Any theories as to how it happened?"

"Estimated time of death is somewhere between eight and ten last night. He probably got shot while he was standing behind the bar, wrote his killer's name on the wall and tried to drag himself out toward the door. Got as far as the living room."

"That's an awful lot for a dying man to do," Ari muttered. "Are they sure he wrote it?"

Ben nodded. "According to the coroner, that name was written by Michael Thorndike himself. They got a nice clear fingerprint at the top of the b. Matched his bloody right hand."

Ari exhaled. If that were true, then it meant Michael Thorndike had used the last of his strength to identify his killer. Bob would be questioned and probably arrested before nightfall.

A young cop approached and spoke with Ben, all the while his eyes shifting from Ben to Ari, who pretended not to notice. She turned away, just as she had done throughout most of her life, every time a guy had come on to her. Except for Bob. Bob had been different.

Ben nodded to Ari and wandered back to the front door with the young cop while Ari took a few steps away and surveyed the crime scene. Things were starting to wind down. The body was being removed and some of the techs were packing up. Ari spotted Molly across the lawn talking to a young black detective. There was no question about who was in charge as Molly pointed at the ground and barked an order. Ari guessed this was Molly's partner and clearly he hadn't done his job correctly. She held up fingers, ticking off a list of things while the man wrote furiously in his notebook. She yelled, "Get it done!" before stomping toward Ari.

"You're free to go, Miss Adams," Molly said curtly, as she walked past Ari. The shades and the attitude were back, and Ari noticed Molly didn't look at her.

Something gnawed at Ari. Once a cop . . .

"Detective," Ari called. Molly stopped and turned abruptly, impatience written into her expression. "Why would Michael Thorndike bother to drag himself out from behind the bar after he wrote Bob's name? It's not like there was a phone out there. And why would he write *Robert*? Most everyone calls Bob Watson, just that, *Bob*."

"We don't know the answer to those questions, Ms. Adams, but I'm sure we'll figure it out. Now, I am going to ask you to leave the crime scene. I know your father is a friend of just about everyone here, but that doesn't give you the right to stick your nose in my investigation," Molly said.

Ari's defenses rose at the mention of Jack Adams. "I think you're forgetting something, Detective. I'm the agent on this house, and I'm legally responsible for this property. My clients are going to want an explanation as to what happened and why part of their five thousand dollar floor must be replaced again."

"Well, all I know is that your friend Mr. Watson better have a good alibi," Molly retorted, her cell phone ringing in her pocket. She scowled as she retrieved it. Beautiful or not, Molly hated amateurs. "If we need anything else we'll be in touch, Ms. Adams," she said before she flipped open the receiver and walked away.

Ari headed to the SUV, Molly's words ringing in her ears. She had no idea how Bob could be implicated in the murder of a Phoenix power magnate, since it was absolutely unbelievable. Yet, it was also too coincidental. Somehow Bob was involved.

She pulled away from the house, a house she had visited hundreds of times during her teenage years. Images of Michael Thorndike's body and the bloody message clouded her mind. She pushed them away, unwilling to contaminate the memories of her youth.

Bob had been the most important person in her life for a long time. They met when he was a high school junior and she a sophomore. They were both on the track team, only mildly aware of the other's existence, until the day they shared a seat on the team bus and became fast friends. Bob wanted more, but Ari brushed him off, like every other guy. He persisted, and Ari finally went out with him a few times and even agreed to go steady. Kissing him had been a chore, but at least with a boyfriend, it was as if a "No Trespassing" sign had been posted on her body, and the boys left her alone. No surprise, really. Bob was the state's number one shot putter—no one would dare mess with his girl. Still, it wasn't right. Ari knew he deserved better.

It amazed her that Bob's manhood remained intact when three months into the relationship, she confessed her suspicions about her sexuality. Most guys would have thrown a fit, blamed her, or played it cool. Instead of destroying their bond, Ari's announcement actually brought them closer, as Bob transformed from boyfriend to counselor. They stayed in touch during college, even though they went to different schools, and Bob married Lily during his senior year. The true proof of friendship, though, came two years later. It was Bob who offered Ari his guest room the night her father disowned her, and it was Bob who had saved her from the biggest mistake of her life.

Chapter Two
Sunday, June 17
6:38 p.m.

Ari accelerated and pulled ahead of the Sunday traffic winding around the base of Camelback Mountain. She was speeding, consciously rushing to Bob before the police could get there. Detective Nelson would not be pleased, but Ari needed to talk to him, not to warn him, but to read his initial expression before he had time to create any facade or erect his defenses. She was Bob's oldest friend, and if anyone could tell if he was lying, it would be Ari.

She glanced in her rearview mirror. The sun was finally setting, and the mountain was awash in red and yellow. This was her favorite time of day. It was still light out, but the burning heat had retreated. The afternoon still didn't seem real, finding Michael Thorndike's body and now Bob possibly accused of murder.

And then there was Molly Nelson, complete with the typical tough cop demeanor Ari thought most of the female cops wore like armor. She had so much to prove and had to be twice as good, probably more so if she was already a detective. Ari admitted she was drawn to her, and she tried to bat the feeling away, but like a pesky fly it kept circling, and she found herself thinking about the tall blond for the third time in an hour. It wasn't just a physical attraction, although Molly was very much Ari's type. No, Ari was drawn to powerful women. She didn't mind that Molly had spoken sharply to her, in fact she knew she deserved it. She got the feeling Molly didn't take any crap from the male officers, but there was something else—she'd seen it in the way the woman had smiled at her when they were alone. There was another side to her, or perhaps many sides and Ari loved women who were complex.

As the SUV drew within a mile of her destination, her thoughts drifted to Bob, a friend who had been there for her during the absolute worst of times. She needed to focus on him, not on her love life.

She turned right on Weatherview and entered the exclusive Arcadia area. Sprawling ranch houses that covered large lots filled with citrus trees, these stately homes were usually owned by doctors, lawyers or CEOs. They were well preserved with manicured yards and good schools—all factors necessary for a quick sale. The competition for these high-priced listings was brutal; everyone who lived there knew a real estate agent and had two or three others soliciting them per week. Obtaining a listing in Arcadia, one of Phoenix's oldest and most prestigious neighborhoods, was quite a coup. Ari had been fortunate to sell a few of these homes during her career, but she knew it was basically a matter of luck and nepotism.

That was how she'd landed Bob and Lily. They already knew her, and they knew they wanted to live in Arcadia, both for the view of Camelback and the status that the name implied. Ari remembered the day Bob and Lily had purchased their house. It had been a series of firsts for both of them—they were her first clients, and this was their first home, bought with Bob's first million. Now, twelve years later, there had been many more millions for Bob, who had a chain of copying centers all over Phoenix.

She wound around the long circular drive, which almost seemed like a trip through a desert garden, and parked next to Bob's Porsche. The woman who answered the door was slim and muscular, her jeans and Oxford cloth shirt outlining her slight frame. "Ari, what a surprise! Please come in," Lily Watson said, flashing a sincere smile.

Ari could hear the NBA commentators as they entered the family room. Bob was glued to the Suns game and didn't notice them at first. "Look who's here, Bob!" Lily announced, her voice competing with the big screen TV.

Bob's attention drifted from the game. When he saw Ari, he lifted his huge frame from the recliner and gave her a bear hug. At thirty-seven, while most of his contemporaries were going to seed, Bob still had the body of a twenty year old. Only his receding hairline betrayed his age. In a moment of vanity on his thirtieth birthday, he'd gone to a hair implant center and asked for plugs. Ari and Lily had arrived just in time, convincing him he would wind up looking like a Seventies lounge lizard. "So, do you have a contract on my parents' house?" he asked playfully.

Ari paused. There was no easy way to say this. She wanted to be sensitive but there wasn't time. "No, Bob. In fact there's a problem. I had a showing this afternoon, and when I walked in, there was a dead body on the floor."

"What?" Lily shrieked.

Bob laughed heartily. "You're joking, right, Ari?"

"No." She watched them closely. They both looked genuinely shocked, unable to process the information. Lily covered her face, and Bob started pacing, his trademark sign of nervousness.

Finally he looked up and asked, "Was it anyone we knew?"

Ari shrugged. "I don't know if you knew him or not. The victim was Michael Thorndike."

Lily gasped and Bob exploded. "Jesus! What the hell is this, Ari?" Her eyes widened in surprise. Lily attempted to rest her hand on Bob's shoulder, but he pushed her away. "What was Michael Thorndike doing in my parents' house?"

Ari shook her head. "I don't know. Is he a friend of yours?"

Bob shot his wife a look of contempt. "Not likely." Silence filled the room and the blaring TV seemed to mock the situation. Bob grabbed the remote and clicked the off button. "I hate that guy. I was going to put a Speedy Copy in this great downtown location, but he caused some major problems and nearly convinced the partnership to lease the property to one of my competitors. If Russ hadn't worked some of his magic on Thorndike, we would have lost the deal." Ari knew Bob's business partner, Russ Swanson, to be extraordinarily diplomatic and level-headed, a nice contrast to Bob's hot-tempered personality.

As if reading her thoughts, Bob added, "That SOB." His face shifted as he realized he was defaming a dead man.

"Bob," Ari interjected, "there's more. Thorndike used his own blood to write your name on the living room wall before he died."

"Oh my God," Lily cried, sinking to the couch.

Total bewilderment covered Bob's face. "Jesus Christ!" Bob boomed. "Why the hell did he do that? The police are going to think I killed him." Bob leaned against the stone fireplace for support, wiping his face with a huge hand. "I just can't believe this!" With one sweeping motion, Bob cleared the mantel, sending pictures, candles and knickknacks to the floor. Lily cried out as glass shattered against the tile.

Ari stepped back, suddenly afraid of Bob's rage. For a moment, all she could see was his size and how easily he could overpower someone like Thorndike. She watched as he turned slowly around, his fists clenched. He stared at the floor, reached down and picked up his wedding photo, the glass cracked in half. Using every ounce of composure he could find, Bob placed it gently back on the mantel. His back still to her, Ari watched the huge man's shoulders move up and down with each breath. She was no longer afraid. He was Bob again.

She moved to him and placed her hand on his shoulder. "Let's try to figure this out," Ari suggested. Bob nodded and Ari motioned for him to sit next to Lily on the couch. Lily moved closer and locked her fingers in his. "Bob, the police are going to ask you for an alibi. The coroner estimates that Michael Thorndike was killed between eight and ten last night. Where were you last evening between those times?"

The couple glanced at each other, and Lily answered. "I was at a charity event. I didn't get home until around eleven. Bob was out at his Tempe store dealing with a problem."

"Were you with anyone?"

"I went out there around six thirty. Kristen was there until eight thirty. She's one of the employees."

"Did anyone come into the store, or did you answer any phone calls after she left?"

Bob searched his memory, but shook his head no. "I was all by myself. I left around ten thirty and came home. No one saw me, and I didn't stop anywhere. That's bad, isn't it?" he asked nervously.

Ari's expression remained neutral. "It would have been helpful if your employee had stayed the entire evening or if someone had seen you during the time the murder was being committed." Bob looked at Lily, whose eyes studied the floor. There was tension between them, but Ari couldn't pinpoint the cause. "You're sure about the times?"

"Yes," he said sharply, aware of the implications. If Kristen had left at eight thirty, Bob still could have driven to central Phoenix and killed Michael Thorndike before ten.

Ari took a deep breath and borrowed one of Detective

Nelson's questions. "Besides the two of you, who else has access to the house?"

Bob and Lily shook their heads. "We're the only people with keys, except for my parents."

"Who else knew you were selling the house?"

Bob sighed. "God, I probably mentioned it to a lot of people. Some just in passing, but there were a few of my business acquaintances who I thought might want to buy it. And you sent a bunch of faxes over, so probably everyone in my office knows, and most of our friends too."

"And I mentioned it to several people at the club and my charity groups, hoping to find a buyer," Lily added.

Ari exhaled. From what they were telling her, many people knew about the vacant house. "When was the last time you saw Michael Thorndike?"

Bob bristled at the name and looked upward trying to remember. "Probably six months ago, when Russ and I went before the League to propose the downtown store. That bastard nearly cost me a fortune."

"Why did he dislike you so much? What did you ever do to him?" Bob glanced at Lily before looking away. When neither of them answered, she knew instantly that Bob had a motive to kill Michael Thorndike and she started to feel sick. "In a little while, the police are probably going to be here. It might be easier to tell a friend first."

"Michael and I had an affair," Lily said softly. "It wasn't very long, but it wasn't just a one-night stand."

"I can't listen to this again," Bob growled. He stalked out of the room, slamming the front door as he exited. The women heard his Porsche revving before he drove away.

Pain swept over Lily's face and tears welled in her eyes. Ari reached for a tissue on the end table and handed it to her, still stunned by Lily's announcement. They sat silently until Lily composed herself enough to continue.

"Bob was working long hours, and I never saw him. I was

21

lonely. Oh, Ari, this all sounds so trite. Bored housewife looking for affection. I wonder now if we should have had children. Maybe I should have pressed . . ." Lily's words faded away with the thought. "Michael and I worked on the same charity committee. He was charming and handsome. I'd heard he could be ruthless in business, but he was so sweet to me. We became close, and I think we had a lot in common. Both of us had spouses who were inattentive. Bob lived at work and all Deborah wanted to do was play tennis at the club. I'd actually met her on several occasions, and we'd been doubles partners a few times. She was definitely a cold one. Anyway, somewhere along the way Michael started to pursue me, and I . . . I responded." Lily's eyes met Ari's. "The truth is, he was the most romantic man I've ever met. I've never told Bob that part," she quickly added with a blush. "I was head over heels in love, Ari," she concluded. A dreamy smile crept on her face, and Ari knew she was reliving the fantasy.

"I take it Bob found out?"

Lily nodded slowly but didn't speak for several seconds. "In the worst way possible. He caught us in bed."

Ari excused herself after asking a few more questions, feeling both dirty and stupid. Granted, she was not a busybody and didn't seek out confidences from friends, although when she was trusted with a secret, it remained just that. She felt as if she'd been plunged into the dark corners of a closet and shown truths she really had no desire to know. Lily and Bob were her friends, and while she was upset to learn that Lily had cheated on Bob, neither had chosen to tell her. She only remembered good times—Bob telling off-colored jokes, Lily's exuberance and friendliness to total strangers at parties and the devotion they seemed to have for each other. That was the image they had projected to Ari, and she was content to see what they wanted her to see.

By the time she got home, she was angry and disappointed that the idyllic picture of the Watsons was ruined. Her thoughts floated to her father, the man who had disappointed her more than anyone else ever could. Ironically, he probably felt she had done the same.

Already feeling the familiar depression creep into her heart, she made a cup of tea and headed straight for the balcony, her retreat from the world. She gazed out at the lights and saw the silhouette of South Mountain in the distance. The view always lightened her mood. She was an urban animal, soaking in the sounds and frenzy of the city, and she loved the fact that she was right in the middle of it, in the heart of central Phoenix, soaring above most everyone on the fifteenth floor. Her chaise lounge was a VIP seat for all the annual parades that marched down Central Avenue, the Fourth of July fireworks at Bolin Plaza, and on a daily basis, the sunsets, which had fascinated her since she was a child. Nothing was more magnificent or humbling.

She sipped her ginseng and contemplated the climactic moment of Lily's story. When Bob burst in on Lily and Thorndike, he pulled the man from the bed and threatened to kill him. Then he stormed out, refusing to come home. It took Lily three months and countless therapy sessions to get her husband back. She shouldered the full blame, not ever mentioning how inattentive Bob had been before the affair. Their marriage improved, and now it seemed rock solid. But was Ari missing the truth now as she obviously had missed in the past?

She rubbed her forehead, as if to dislodge a thought that wouldn't come. Something was bothering her, but she couldn't put her finger on it. The phone interrupted her thoughts. "Hello?"

"Maybe you don't understand my English," a terse female voice announced.

Ari sat straight up. "Is that how you always start a conversation, Detective Nelson?"

"I don't have time for pleasantries, Ms. Adams." Molly seethed across the line.

"What's the matter?"

"Bob Watson is missing, and according to his wife, you paid them a visit late this afternoon during which time he left the house and hasn't been seen since."

Ari's mouth went dry. When Bob sped off, she assumed that he would return soon. It was his nature to take flight instead of fight. She could remember countless times he had stormed out of a room, but he was a volcano, erupting and going dormant. That was his pattern. Now it was eleven o'clock, and he should have been back, if he was coming back.

"Ms. Adams, are you listening to me?"

"Yes, Detective, every word. I did go to see them this afternoon, and discuss the damage to the property. Bob and Lily Watson are acting as the trustees of the property."

Ari hoped her business-like attitude might deflect some of Molly's hostility.

Molly sighed. "And that's the *only* reason you went over there? Do you really think I'm going to believe that?" she asked, her voice shrill.

Ari was glad miles separated them, because if the detective had been in close proximity, she sounded as though she would strangle Ari. "You just happened to stop by after learning Bob Watson was accused of murder for a friendly chat? How stupid do you think I am? And am I supposed to believe that you just kept the discussion confined to painting and flooring?"

"Well . . ."

"I'm sure a bloody floor would be plenty of reason for Bob Watson to flee," Molly added sarcastically. "Maybe he's drowning his sorrows at a bar somewhere, terribly upset that he lost a sale!" Ari closed her mouth and just let the detective rant. "I suppose you know all about Michael Thorndike's affair with Mrs. Watson. And how it almost ruined their marriage?"

"Yes," Ari answered honestly, "we discussed that. But that was resolved a long time ago. They went to therapy and Bob forgave

Lily for cheating on him. I think it shows a lot of character to be able to forgive your wife, even when you catch her in bed with her lover." Ari couldn't help but defend Bob to this woman who seemed to want to throw him in jail. The other end was silent for a while, and Ari wondered if Molly had hung up. "Are you still there, Detective?"

When Molly answered, it was slow and deliberate. "That part I didn't know. Bob Watson actually found his wife in bed with Michael Thorndike?"

Ari's hand clenched the receiver. "I thought Lily told you that."

"No."

"Well, I was told that in confidence," Ari sputtered, "as a friend."

"Let me tell you something, Ms. Adams. I'm not your friend. I'm a cop and this is a homicide investigation. So if you have any other information that could be useful in solving this crime I need to know about it right now." Molly paused and waited. Ari was certain the detective didn't know about Bob's threat. "Well?" Molly barked.

Ari pursed her lips. A lie was forming, and she was about to say something when Molly roared, "Because of your interference, our prime suspect has disappeared. If you do not stay out of this investigation, I will have you arrested!" The phone slammed down in Ari's ear.

She closed her eyes, letting her emotions swirl inside. The police would hunt for Bob. He certainly had motive, both personal and professional, and he had the opportunity. It looked very simple, but Bob's reaction that afternoon was sheer shock, and Ari had only seen him like that once before. She was certain Bob Watson was telling the truth, and even if it meant going to jail, she would help her friend—if she could find him.

Chapter Three
Sunday, June 17
10:05 p.m.

Ordering the fourth shot of whiskey was a mistake. Molly passed from happily buzzed to somewhat incoherent. She shifted on the stool, catching the eye of a hungry redhead who raised her eyebrows in question. All she had to do was nod and she wouldn't be alone tonight in her small, empty apartment. She let her eyes drop to the polished bar. She was tired. Tired of her life. Too many one-night stands, too many women and way too much drinking. Her life was like a terminally ill patient whom Molly had given up on a long time ago. Her failed relationships lined up in her mind, each of her lovers leaving with a door slam louder than the one previous. Rachel, her last partner and a fellow cop, had cracked the jamb.

Rehashing it made her crave another drink. She held up her

hand, but Vicki, Hideaway's favorite bartender, scowled and waved her off. Molly had to give her credit. The woman kept her in line and knew her limit, but this was Hideaway, the premier lesbian bar in Phoenix. The bartenders knew their regulars and knew how to keep them as regulars. Even on Sunday night, the place had a pulse. All of the bar stools were occupied, and a handful of women were bopping to the dance music. Most of the outer booths were empty, the patrons choosing to cluster together like a flock. Molly knew most of them by name and what size panties each wore. She'd slept with every woman who frequented Hideaway, mostly as one-night stands.

She motioned to Vicki for a glass of water and worked to sober up—it would be par for the day if she got a DUI. Inheriting the Michael Thorndike murder was the captain's way of breaking her. She'd been hired by his predecessor and that was the first strike against her. Being the only lesbian detective was another, and her abrasive personality was the last. During her last evaluation, she'd been encouraged to "foster better social skills and peer communication." In her opinion, she communicated just fine, letting many of her male co-workers know that she wouldn't tolerate the traditional sexual harassment. She hated the good old boy network. It had been tough on the Spokane police force but Phoenix was worse.

Molly returned to the case at hand, very grateful that Michael Thorndike was discovered on a Sunday. By the time the press dogs had picked up the scent, the crime scene was secured and the body removed. So far, the crime scene yielded few clues. The bar's countertop had been wiped clean as well as the broken patio door, save Ari's thumb print. Hopefully, the lab results would glean some evidence, but she doubted there would be a smoking gun. They could have used one since the weapon was missing.

In hindsight, Molly should have opted to visit Deborah Thorndike, the grieving widow, but instead she gave that assignment to her partner, a rookie she didn't quite trust yet. So while

Andre had been doling out empathy and drinking iced tea on the Thorndike's sun porch, Molly had been dodging daggers from Lily Watson at her front door and learning her husband had fled, a fact that seemed to please Lily somewhat. Ari's previous visit had primed Lily for a fight, and she acted hostile and defensive toward Molly, responding to questions with clipped, terse answers and allowing the detective only to cross the threshold.

She glanced at the redhead who was still staring at her. The woman licked her lips, and Molly got an excellent view of her tongue ring. Molly started to stand up, her decision made, when her cell phone vibrated in her pocket. She quickly exited to a hallway, escaping the pounding music.

"Nelson."

"Gee, Detective, it's nice to know you're out on the town while our prime suspect is missing!"

Molly moved further down the hallway toward the emergency exit, but Captain Ruskin had already made his point. "There's nothing more I can do tonight, Captain. We've got Watson's house under watch and a File Stop out for him and that Porsche. I'm sure he'll turn up."

"Aren't women always the optimists," Ruskin cracked. "I hope for your sake he does, Nelson. This is your ass. You let a homicide suspect slip through your fingers. I don't understand how the hell that happened but you better find him or else you'll be pulling third shift in Maryvale."

The loud click ended the conversation before Molly could say another word. She unclenched her teeth and took a deep breath. The case wasn't a day old and already it was a disaster, a ticking bomb sitting in her lap, ready to explode and blow her career into pieces.

She wanted another drink, but there was no way Vicki would serve her again. Maybe she and the redhead could stop at a minimart on the way. She made her way back toward the music, imagining the redhead going down on her, tongue stud and all, but the woman was gone.

Molly climbed into her truck and headed home. Crossing Central Avenue, she glanced right at the series of parallel lights that climbed toward the sky. According to her witness statement, Ari Adams lived in one of those condos. The thought of the woman made Molly's blood boil and her face flush at the same time. If Ari hadn't beaten her to the Watson's house, they would have Bob in custody. He'd had no intention of running, which, Molly admitted made his guilt questionable. But once Ari had spoken to him, he was gone, and now Captain Ruskin was breathing down her neck. If he found out that Ari had tampered with the crime scene and warned Bob Watson about the arrival of the police, he would surely have her arrested. She snorted. If she did have to arrest Ari for obstructing an investigation, she'd have to take her straight to her bedroom instead of a jail cell.

Now there was a woman who wouldn't be a one-night stand. She was too refined and sophisticated, definitely above something meaningless and cheap. She replayed their meeting at the crime scene and the way Ari sat perched in the SUV, poised like a model, tucking that random strand of hair behind her ear. When Molly had reached for Ari's arm and taken her elbow, the physical contact sent a surge through Molly that surprised and overwhelmed her. Only when Ari asked her to let go did she even realize they were still connected. More powerful than the touch was Ari's breathy voice, totally seductive.

Molly knew she didn't stand a chance with Ari. An Elle McPherson businesswoman would never be seen on the arm of a lowly civil servant the size of a Chicago Bears lineman. Not likely, and probably not gay either if she really thought about it. Still, when Ari had smiled at her, she felt her knees go weak. Ari

29

hadn't noticed Molly leaning against the side of the SUV for support, all the while smiling back at her like an idiot.

Pulling into her parking space this late always sent a pang of loneliness through her chest. She hated living alone, but she'd resolved that after her last breakup, she wouldn't jump into a relationship with just anybody. For the last year she had confined herself to meaningless sexual encounters, rationalizing them as worthy substitutes for love.

The answering machine blinked incessantly and a brilliant red number 2 shone above the light. She poured herself a whiskey, slapped the playback button and sat down at her piano. Her fingers glided across the keys, playing softly while the tape clicked several times. Molly made her ninetieth mental note to invest in voice mail.

Her brother Brian filled the room with his deep baritone. "Hey sis, how's it going? Saw you on the news tonight. You were pointing and barking orders at some poor cop. Naw, I'm just kidding, you looked very professional. I hope you're not still at work, but I'll bet you are. Let's get together and chat. Sorry I missed you." Molly was sorry too. She was closest to Brian, mainly because they were both the black sheep, and they shared the same fiery temperament.

The machine beeped once more and a woman cleared her throat. "Detective Nelson, I hope you don't mind that I called you at home. I tried the precinct, but they said you had already left." Molly instantly recognized Ari Adams's seductive voice. She rushed to the machine and leaned close. "I won't tell you how I got your home phone number. I doubt you'd approve . . . it wasn't exactly illegal, just maybe a tad questionable . . . but I guess you already know that sometimes I push the bounds of what is ethical," Ari said with a slight giggle. "Anyway, I know I'm rambling, but I just felt so bad about Bob Watson running off. I had no idea that he would react like that, but I still think he's innocent. I'm really sorry that it came back on you—I'm sure

David Ruskin was a total asshole. Oh, sorry about the swearing. It's just a really appropriate description of him, don't you think?" Molly laughed out loud, totally agreeing. How did Ari know Ruskin? Probably because of her father. "Well, that's all I wanted to say. I'm just really sorry. Oh, and in case you don't recognize my voice, this is Ari Adams. Bye."

A shrill sound announced the end of Molly's messages. She replayed Ari's five times, twice just to make sure she caught everything and three more times to hear Ari's voice.

Molly returned to the piano and propped Michael Thorndike's murder file on the music stand. Her fingers drifted across the keys as she scanned the day's notes. On the surface, the case seemed simple. Michael Thorndike was helpful enough to leave the most incriminating clue—the name of his killer. Bob Watson certainly had a motive, and a shaky alibi at best, one her partner would check out first thing in the morning.

Still, it seemed too staged. Why had Thorndike's body been in the living room? And while it didn't look good for Bob Watson, Ari was adamant that he couldn't be a killer. Thinking of Ari again, she played more forcefully, creating a new melody, one that was rather good. She had no idea where she was going—it was like an unplanned night drive, but she'd done it for so long, that she just had to follow the notes. Once in a while, Molly would create something brilliant, but she never wrote anything down. How many best-selling hits had literally slipped through her fingers?

Next door, her neighbor Mrs. Lyons clicked off her TV. The eighty-three year old liked to stay up late and watch *The Tonight Show*. That Jay Leno wasn't nearly as good as Johnny Carson, but he did his best. Music flowed through the walls. Mrs. Lyons didn't mind Molly's music and she liked the idea that a police woman lived next door. Yet she could always tell when the detective was upset, such as tonight. The music captivated her, but it had a sad, forlorn tone—all of Molly's best compositions did.

She knew Molly would play for at least another half hour and gradually the notes would become so soft that she couldn't hear them anymore. And then, perhaps, the detective would go to bed for a well-deserved sleep.

Chapter Four
Monday, June 18
8:00 a.m.

At eight in the morning, Molly's day was already three hours old, having arrived early to process the paperwork for some of her other cases—people who didn't rate as highly as Michael Thorndike, at least not in the eyes of Captain David Ruskin. The death of a civic leader was top priority, and Molly would spend as much time as necessary to catch his killer, even if it meant other homicides would go cold.

By three, she'd already clocked ten hours, a figure that would probably double before she went home. A yawn escaped her lips about the same time her stomach rumbled in protest for skipping lunch. She glanced at her watch for the third time in five minutes and crossed her legs, trying to find comfort while she waited for members the infamous Phoenix League to grace her with their presence. Molly felt like a folded trundle bed sitting on the uncomfortable visitor's chair. She stared enviously at the five leather office chairs spread around the conference table in front of her, each one complete with back support and rounded arms. She debated whether to claim the fifth one for herself. Its executive wouldn't be returning. Michael Thorndike's death brought the partnership down to four, as she pictured the executives bantering ideas about. A large print hung over the credenza that looked like a paint splatter, but Molly didn't know anything about art. The rest of the room was sterile and plain. She guessed the partners kept the really good stuff in their offices.

The door clicked and the quartet paraded in. Strength in numbers, or none of them trusted each other enough to be left alone with a detective. Molly quickly assessed their well-tailored and perfectly groomed figures, her first impressions setting like cement. Three men and one woman, all roughly in their mid-forties. All white. She wasn't surprised. None of them bothered to offer any kind of greeting, and instead they retreated behind the conference table, using it as a shield. Molly realized that their combined net worth probably could pay half of the police force for a year.

They each wore a stern expression. Only Cyril Lemond looked remotely friendly, a half-smile on his thin lips and his hands clasped in front of him on the table. Molly watched him closely, as he was the only one without a concrete alibi on the night of Thorndike's murder, and he lived just a block from the murder site.

"Detective Nelson, how can we help you?" Lemond's place at the center identified him as the leader. Molly scanned the other partners, their faces blank. She guessed Felix Trainor, the man at the end of the table, carried the least amount of clout. Undoubtedly, Lemond would be the mouthpiece.

Too uncomfortable and tired to play games, Molly got right

to the point. "I need some specific information about Michael Thorndike's business dealings. Since you are his partners, I thought you could shed some light on his recent projects, future projects . . ." She let her voice trail off in hopes that they understood. She was sure they did, even though they didn't seem to want to.

Civility gushed from Lemond's face. "And you think this might have some bearing on his death?"

Molly went for the jugular. "Mr. Lemond, most homicide victims are killed for money or love. I've got the love part covered, but this is the money end." Molly made a sweeping gesture at the five thousand dollar conference table.

Lemond's smile flickered slightly. "We'd be more than happy to cooperate with you, Detective."

"Good." Once again, Molly resituated her large frame and pulled out her notes. "Please tell me about Mr. Thorndike's business ventures."

A staged cough erupted from Felix Trainor's corner. Lemond's eyes signaled permission. When Trainor spoke, his voice was hesitant and careful. "Michael was exploring possibilities with the Emporium. He wanted to make it into a premier museum like the Getty Center."

Molly was surprised. "The Emporium? I thought you all worked exclusively in Phoenix?"

"Michael saw tremendous potential," Trainor quickly stated, eyeing his partners.

Molly made a note. Many developers had tried and failed to "realize the Emporium's potential." Located in downtown Scottsdale, it had worn many hats—office space, retail shops, IMAX theater, even a site for the traveling Smithsonian. Nothing seemed to stick. The Emporium was Scottsdale's white elephant. Turning it around would have made Thorndike a hero, Molly thought to herself.

"Some of us don't share Michael's *vision*," the female partner said, coming to life. "It was a bad investment idea, and it could have sunk us."

Felix Trainor leaned forward. "Michael's plan would have worked, Florence."

Molly remembered the woman's name, Florence Denman. Her face colored, and she glared at Trainor. He'd be in severe trouble for contradicting Lady Steel, as she was known in the business community. Judging from the obvious cosmetic surgery done to her face, *steel* wouldn't have been the nickname Molly chose.

"You're as disillusioned as Michael was, Felix," Florence concluded. "I'm sorry he's dead," she announced without any sympathy, "but at least we won't lose anymore money chasing Don Quixote's windmills." She snorted. "An art museum! What an idea!"

"I'm sure Detective Nelson didn't come here to listen to our petty squabbling," Cyril Lemond interjected. Molly wondered if petty squabbling included murder. Trainor slumped into his seat while Denman visibly fumed. Lemond played the diplomat. "As you can see, Detective, we are all vehement with our opinions and feel comfortable sharing and discussing differences."

The euphemisms poured from his mouth. Spin doctoring was Lemond's art. Molly paused, pretending to shift gears. "Was Mr. Thorndike involved in any other projects?"

The partners looked at each other and shrugged. The man to Lemond's left who, if she remembered correctly from her notes, was Sorrel Whitlock. He looked utterly bored and Molly guessed he had the least knowledge of Thorndike's affairs.

Again, it was Felix Trainor who spoke up. "Michael liked to focus on one thing at a time. You know, shine his light at one target, to maximize the possibility for success."

Molly withheld a heavy sigh and wrote "pompous ass" in her notes next to his name. "So this was his only project?" Everyone nodded. Molly focused on Cyril Lemond. "How did you feel about the Emporium idea, Mr. Lemond?"

Lemond's eyes shifted to the wall. He inhaled before meeting Molly's gaze. "I would have to say it had potential, but Michael hadn't thought it through yet. Now we will never know." The last part was said with a touch of finality and Molly knew her little interview was about to end.

"Can any of you think of anyone who would want to kill Michael Thorndike?"

The room exploded in laughter.

Chapter Five
Monday, June 18
9:01 a.m.

Since Ari didn't answer to anyone, her day started much later and much differently from Molly's. She called Lily after her morning shower. In a shotgun delivery, Lily announced Bob had not returned, she had no idea where he was, she'd called all their friends and acquaintances, she was terribly distraught, and Molly Nelson was a class-A bitch, showing up at her house with a search warrant at seven in the morning. Ari hung up, having said nothing except hello.

Her pager went off precisely at 9:01, announcing the official end of the weekend. She had an offer on one of her listings waiting for her prompt attention. Realizing there was nothing else she could do for Bob at the moment, she fought the morning traffic to her office at Allstar Realty.

Leaving the Tucson PD had sent Ari reeling. She never planned on any life but law enforcement. Consequently, she couldn't visualize herself in another career. She lacked the skills, interest or education for every profession suggested by friends and family. As a believer in providence, she put her future in its hands and waited, all the while living off her meager savings. Three months later she was starting to lose hope until one morning she opened the newspaper and read an article about the predicted housing boom in Phoenix. She enrolled in real estate school before finishing her coffee. Providence proved correct and after twelve years, Ari was now a seasoned veteran and associate broker at thirty-three. Like most agents, she was self-employed and kept her own hours. For a monthly fee, Allstar provided all of the necessary office equipment and receptionists who fielded the incoming calls and paged the agents when necessary. It was a convenient setup, and Ari liked everything about her job—except the managing broker, the only person who had any authority over Ari's professional life. Still, she could endure him on most days, since she only had to see him at office meetings.

The paperwork and follow-up calls quickly ate up the morning. When Ari finally looked at the clock, it was noon, and a brunette bombshell was sashaying toward her, hips swinging from side to side like a supermodel. Ari waved at Jane Frank, her best friend and colleague. Both men and women turned their heads at the sight of her perfectly coifed shoulder length hair and painted China doll face. It was no surprise to Ari that Jane had fended off several marriage proposals from both sexes.

Jane and Ari had dated for exactly one hour and twenty-six minutes, concluding halfway through their first date that they were totally incompatible. Although they were both certainly attractive, Ari's Mediterranean beauty was derived from genetics while Jane's depended on bottles, tubes and compacts. She knew every sales clerk at Neiman-Marcus and drove a Lexus, whereas

Ari much preferred jeans, no makeup and her SUV. They were opposites who made great friends but could never be lovers.

Jane noticed Ari packing her files away. "Heading out a little early. Got a hot date?"

Ari blushed, thinking momentarily of Molly Nelson. "No, I've got some things to do," Ari answered casually.

A knowing smile crossed Jane's face. "I imagine you're gonna need a lot of Pine Sol to get the blood out of those floorboards."

"Shh!" Ari cautioned. She shut the door. "How did you know?"

"They flashed a shot of the house on TV and I saw your sign." Jane flicked a lint ball from her Dior jacket. "C'mon, tell me all about it. You know I always wanted to be a Charlie's Angel." Jane extended her fingers like a gun.

Ari grinned as Jane shot down an invisible enemy. "Jane, Charlie's Angels didn't worry about breaking a nail."

"No," Jane disagreed. "I'll bet you money Cheryl Ladd's manicure was always perfect. That woman had style." Jane waved a finger at Ari. "Don't change the subject," she ordered. "I'm in no mood for idle chit-chat when good gossip looms. Tell me about yesterday right now or I'll go to the press and spread an ugly rumor that you're straight."

"Now there's a threat," Ari said, rolling her eyes. She dropped into a chair and barreled through the events of the last day, describing the dead body, her encounter with the sexy detective and, finally, Lily's affair and Bob's disappearance.

"You know who you should talk to is Bob's partner, Russ Swanson. If Lily doesn't know where Bob is, Russ might."

Ari nodded. "Lily's already called him. She got the same answer I did this morning—he's not in." She shifted in her chair. "How do you know Russ Swanson?"

"I have my ways," Jane said slyly, examining her perfect manicure.

Ari wasn't sure if Jane was telling the truth or just playing for attention, a typical Jane habit. She could shovel a load of bs, but she also had dirt on a lot of people. "Well?" Ari said impatiently, "are you going to tell me?"

Jane raised an eyebrow. "Did you know Russ is family?"

Ari's jaw dropped. "What? How do you know this?"

"He hangs out at Smiley's all the time, at the bar. He's a regular."

"A lot of straight people go to Smiley's," Ari remarked. While it was one of the few gay owned restaurants in Phoenix, straight people appreciated the decor and the great food.

"True, but since I've watched him put his hand in another man's back pocket, I think I can make the assumption."

Ari digested this fact. She knew Russ as an acquaintance, merely as a link to Bob. They saw each other at parties sometimes, but Ari knew very little about the man except what Bob had told her: he was an exceptional businessman, very shrewd with money and could make things happen, even in the most unlikely of situations.

"Thanks for the tip," Ari said, rising to leave. She snapped up her briefcase and headed out the door, leaving Jane standing there with her hands on her hips.

"Please be careful," she warned. "You know, we're really not Charlie's Angels and they never got hurt because there had to be a show the next week."

Ari waved good-bye and took off. Her stomach churned, a result of hunger and stress. She pulled into a hamburger drive-in, ordered and scribbled notes while she ate. Assuming Bob was innocent, why did the killer want to frame him? How did the killer lure Michael Thorndike to Bob's parents' house, especially on a Saturday night? And most importantly, why had Michael Thorndike dragged himself out from behind the bar and into the living room? She pictured the floor plan in her mind and saw the area behind the bar. There was something about that wall . . .

It would come eventually, at least that's what her dad always said. She had thought more about her father in the last twenty-four hours than in months. He'd retired two years before and moved to Oregon. "Fishing country," he called it. Here she was replaying scenes from her life that up until yesterday, she had successfully blocked out of her memory. Now, pieces of her childhood were coming back, fragments she assumed were lost forever.

When her father was working a case, he would pace on the porch endlessly, sometimes talking to himself and gesturing. She would watch from her window, trying to read his lips and praying he would look up and motion for her to come down—something that never happened.

She brushed the memories away and caught Highway 51 downtown. Her father had given her one good piece of advice—he'd told her if she stayed out of trouble and on the high road, there was a ninety-five percent chance that she wouldn't be murdered by someone she knew. Not bad advice from a homicide detective.

Michael Thorndike's life was anywhere but the high road. From what Ari knew of him, he had countless enemies and few people would mourn his death, including his widow. But then again, her name hadn't been written in blood ten feet from his dead body.

A few taps on the library computer yielded more than a hundred references to his name, many of them in the last twenty-four hours since the announcement of his murder. Every power broker in Phoenix was watching and commenting. Even the governor was assuring the public that justice would be served. The pressure on Molly would be enormous and she couldn't imagine where Bob could be hiding, unseen and unnoticed. Bob's picture was plastered all over the Internet and on the front page of the *Arizona Republic*. How could he stay hidden for long?

Ari spent three more hours scrolling through newspaper articles that detailed Michael Thorndike's career. He was a multi-millionaire, most of his fortune made from his land developments. For as often as he'd been investigated, he should have had his own parking space down at the courts building. Words like ruthless, hated and unethical kept appearing on the screen. She knew, however, that the string of wronged business associates probably would account for a low turnout at the funeral and nothing more. That shortened the list of suspects greatly.

Ari wasn't surprised to find an entire Web site devoted to the Phoenix League, especially its hero and star, Michael Thorndike. Convinced that the downtown area could be more than office space, Thorndike had organized a group of business entrepreneurs who shared his vision. At first, everyone scoffed. During the weekdays, high priced attorneys, government employees and curious tourists filled the sidewalks, but sunset signaled the exodus, turning the area into a ghost town. Only the shadows of the homeless and the drug dealers were visible then. The ten square city blocks were the most dangerous and feared at night. It even carried the nickname "The Deuce" since no one made the mistake of coming downtown at night twice.

Michael Thorndike vowed to change all of that. Amidst the huge glass skyscrapers, he envisioned theaters, sports facilities, shops and more restaurants than the rest of the city combined. With their own financing and some strong-arm tactics, the Phoenix League planted the seeds of urban growth. Others jumped on the bandwagon, the masses of bulldozers appeared and the investors tripled their money in two years. During the process, the homeless and some vintage businesses were unfairly displaced in the name of progress and the greater good.

From the fifth floor of the library, Ari gazed through the huge glass windows at the League's results. Sandwiched between the skyscrapers, Banc One Ballpark, America West Arena, and the

43

Herberger Theatre assured Thorndike and company of a profit as throngs of people were lured downtown for sports and culture. At the corner of Fillmore and 7th Street sat the Arizona Center, Phoenix's only outdoor mall and the home of the Phoenix League. Staring at the chrome and copper tower, Ari gathered her printouts and headed out. She didn't have an appointment and she didn't have any idea what she could possibly learn from walking into Thorndike's office, but she just wanted to be closer to what represented Michael Thorndike, a person she was sure wasn't entirely depicted in the sanitized news accounts.

She crossed the courtyard that divided the mall from the League's building, passing a hotdog cart. A short, wiry black man with graying hair held out a foot long dog, complete with chili, relish and onions. Red stitching across the pocket identified the vendor as "Joe," and his grin was short a few teeth.

"Care for a Coney?" he offered, his toothless smile expanding.

Ari paused, her stomach pleading with her to stop for a late afternoon snack but her feet carried her forward. "I'll be back, Joe. Save one for me." Joe nodded, still smiling.

The Phoenix League's executive suites inhabited the entire top floor. Ari's loafers sunk into the plush carpet as she stepped out of the elevator and into a small foyer. A long hallway stood between her and the receptionist, every office's first line of defense.

The woman didn't notice Ari, her view obstructed by a large, black wreath on a stand and her hands busily directing the phone traffic. Ari moved in line with the wreath, trying to stay unnoticed for as long as possible. She studied the gallery of photographs along the walls. Many were aerial shots of the buildings financed by the League interspersed with photos of the partners breaking ground and shaking hands with city officials and other business gurus.

Michael Thorndike was definitely the most attractive of the partners, his winning smile filling the frames. The hall ended and Ari found herself in front of a mammoth cherry wood desk and the young, perky receptionist. Her ruby lips formed a complimentary smile that she undoubtedly dispensed two or three dozen times a day. It was a wordless inquiry that demanded to know, "What the hell do you want?"

Ari worked up a plausible lie. "Hello. I'm with *The New Times* and we were hoping for a quote from one of Mr. Thorndike's associates."

Like a robot, the brunette shook her head before Ari had punctuated her sentence. "I'm sorry that won't be possible." Ari instantly realized she had a better chance of catching typhoid than she did getting past this receptionist.

Feigning disappointment, Ari looked at the wreath and noticed a framed photo situated in the middle. It was an old eight-by-ten of Michael Thorndike during his college baseball days, squatting in the batter's box. The photo was titled "Lefty." A chord struck in Ari's brain. She stared at the photo until a familiar voice floated out from somewhere behind the receptionist.

"Excuse me," Ari murmured, already heading toward the elevator. Surprised at the ease with which her refusal was met, the receptionist narrowed her brow and watched Ari depart.

Ari pounded on the elevator button. The familiar voice belonged to Molly Nelson who was standing in front of the receptionist's desk, speaking to a man obviously showing her out. If the detective caught her, she would probably Mirandize her, although it would almost be worth it just to spend some more time with Molly. Ari's eyes flicked between the detective and the elevator numbers slowly counting up to reach the top floor.

Molly was clearly trying to exit, taking a few steps away from her host, saying all of those little closing remarks that people use to end conversations. Thank goodness, Ari thought, this businessman was a talker. She heard Molly make a final good-bye just as the elevator opened. Ari pressed against the wall, frantically jamming the button for the ground floor. When the doors finally shut, Ari caught her breath. She'd narrowly escaped Molly's wrath, but she'd found an important clue—she just didn't know what it was.

Heat radiated from the concrete outside. Her body adjusted from the building's ice cold air conditioning to the sweltering summer afternoon. She retreated to the shade of the hotdog cart as Joe grinned and plopped a Coney in front of her. She stood there chomping on the dog, waiting for the confrontation that would most likely occur when Molly came out. She wasn't going to sprint across the mall to avoid the detective. This was a public place and she had every right to be here. In fact, she found herself excited at the prospect of talking with Molly again. A few moments later, the heavy glass doors opened and Molly trudged down the sidewalk. Her shoulders were hunched and she seemed to carry the weight of the world. She headed straight for Ari.

"Ms. Adams, what an unexpected coincidence," Molly said sarcastically. Her eyes shifted from Ari to the confused hotdog vendor.

"You want a Coney Island?" Ari asked between mouthfuls. "This is great, Joe." Joe nodded, still unsure about the tension between the two women. He'd given up trying to figure out the female sex long ago. He just did what his wife told him and everything was fine.

Molly continued her hard stare but she didn't say no. Ari motioned to Joe who busied himself creating an edible peace offering.

"Why are you here?" Molly's voice was flat.

"I'm just shopping," Ari offered with a shrug. She paid Joe

and handed Molly the hotdog and a soda. The women moved to a bench away from the mall traffic. Ari finished her last few bites and watched Molly. Even eating, her body was rigid, her jaw tense and Ari could see the strain in her neck muscles.

"Did you get my message?"

"Yes," Molly growled, her mouth chewing the last bite. She gulped the last of her drink, pitched all the trash into a nearby garbage can and leaned over Ari. "I'm telling you for the last time to stay out of my investigation. I have enough trouble without a junior detective nipping at my heels."

Pride prevented Ari from being truthful. She licked her lips and flashed a killer smile. "Detective, I wasn't interfering—"

"Jesus!" Molly exploded, backing away from the bench. "I don't have time for this, Ari. You think you can flirt with me, and I'll let you hang me out to dry? My job is on the line here. I saw you get on the elevator and the receptionist described you perfectly, so can we cut through the shit?" Ari looked away, ashamed and embarrassed by her behavior. Molly unconsciously balled her hands into fists, yet another sign of her tension.

"This is all a game to you! What does your father think of his daughter snooping around like some wannabe private eye? Doesn't he worry you'll get hurt? I would think, if anything, he would understand the potential danger, not to mention the fact that you are seriously jeopardizing my investigation."

It was a slap across the face in more ways than Molly could know. Ari wanted to scream that the last time she'd spoken to her father was at her mother's funeral, three years ago. Instead, she used all of her energy to blink away the tears. Regaining her composure, she rose slowly from the bench and started to walk away.

Molly's breath caught in her throat. Had she seen tears in Ari's eyes? "Ari!" Molly called, sprinting to catch up with her. "Ari, I just don't understand why you're doing this," she said in a kind voice.

"Bob is my friend," she answered, her pace still brisk. She had to get to her car. She could handle Molly's bitchy attitude, but when the detective was tender and compassionate, she wanted to melt.

Still, Molly pressed on. "I know that. But is that enough of a reason to jeopardize an investigation, to get yourself in trouble? And what if he did do it? Can you really live with yourself knowing you helped a murderer?"

"He's not a murderer!" Ari proclaimed, suddenly stopping and facing Molly. "He didn't do it," Ari emphasized. "Molly, I've known Bob for most of my life. We have a very special relationship, and I believe in his innocence."

Ari's passion touched Molly. She placed her hands gently on Ari's shoulders before she spoke. "Then let me do my job."

"I will. But I can't see Bob go to jail for something he didn't do."

"Do you know where he is, Ari?" Molly asked, her eyes probing Ari's for the truth.

"No," Ari answered honestly.

"But if you did, would you tell me?" Ari hesitated and Molly shook her head. "Then I have to think I can't trust you."

"I'm sorry. But you don't get it."

Molly threw up her hands and sighed. They stared at each other, unable to resolve their differences. "I guess there's nothing else to say," Molly concluded. She turned to walk away.

"Molly, wait," Ari said. Molly faced her and she could see Ari was searching for words and tears were coming down her face. Finally she asked, "Have you ever owed a debt you never thought you could repay?"

Chapter Six
Monday, June 18
8:16 p.m.

If Molly needed any other reminders of her botched confrontation with Ari, the Coney Island gave her heartburn for the rest of the day. She nursed a bottle of antacid while her partner, Andre Williams, detailed his interview with Kristen Duke, Bob Watson's employee. Molly shifted in her desk chair, absorbing Andre's impressions of Kristen—young, rebellious and difficult to read. Andre himself was only a handful of years older than the witness, and Molly questioned his objectivity and opinions.

She and Williams were polar opposites. Dressed in a crisp, white shirt and pressed gray pants, he looked more like a Wall Street trader than a cop. They would never bump into each other at a store since Molly doubted Andre had ever seen the inside of a Kmart, the only place she shopped. As he talked he gestured and his college ring caught her eye. The shiny gold stood out against his chocolate brown skin. She couldn't help but feel he was shoving the ring in her face, a reminder of her lack of a college diploma. They did have one thing in common: they were the only two minority detectives in the division. Molly thought it was less than coincidental that the black man and the lesbian had been thrown together.

"Let me get this straight," she reviewed, more for Andre's benefit than her own. "Kristen Duke says she was at the Speedy Copy until eight thirty."

Andre glanced at his notes, not wanting to misquote in front of Molly. "Right. At which time Miss Duke left Mr. Watson there and went home to a townhouse on Hardy that she shares with two other coeds."

Molly quickly calculated in her head. "That still left time for Watson to get back to central Phoenix and kill Thorndike. Did you interview the roommates?"

He frowned. "No, I didn't see the point. They aren't the suspects."

"It's called follow-through! Interview the girls tomorrow," Molly snapped.

Andre nodded and scribbled a reminder. He knew better than to argue with Molly. They were partners, but she was certainly more experienced.

"I also finished canvassing the neighbors, but no one claims to have heard anything, and no one saw anything. Most everyone seemed to be out."

Molly shook her head, not surprised. The murder had occurred on a Saturday night, and even if anyone had heard a shot, they would have discounted it. Such was the case of city living.

"What about Lily Watson?" she asked.

"She was at a charity function. Several people saw her at dinner."

"When was dinner?"

Andre rifled through some pages. "Six o'clock."

"What about after that?"

Andre fidgeted uncomfortably and finally met Molly's seething stare. He suddenly longed for his former life as a patrolman. "I'll double-check," he said. And before she could ask, he volunteered, "I also spoke with the people at the movie theater. A guy running one of the cash registers remembered the deceased's wife, Deborah Thorndike. He even knew that she bought a large popcorn and Diet Coke."

Molly sighed. "Great. Nobody killed Michael Thorndike." She closed her eyes, trying to remain patient. She'd been a rookie, too, she reminded herself. But she certainly didn't remember being this incompetent. When Andre didn't resume the conversation, she barked, "Don't you have something you could be doing?" He jumped up and darted out the door.

Molly groaned. She'd gained little from her trip downtown. There were still no leads on Bob Watson, and Deborah Thorndike had dismissed her after five minutes, claiming she was too distraught at the moment to be questioned again. All Molly had learned was that Thorndike had been at home alone working, refusing to join his wife at the movies.

It was a crappy day, and she'd taken out her frustrations on other people, a character flaw she desperately needed to improve. Her eyes wandered to the newspaper on the desk. Michael Thorndike's face stared at her from the front page. She'd found it on her chair earlier in the day, and Captain Ruskin had circled Thorndike's picture several times in red marker. The message was succinct and clear.

Molly closed her eyes and leaned back in her chair. Her cell phone chirped in her pocket, and she smiled when she saw the name on Caller ID.

"Hey," she offered casually.

"Hey yourself, sis."

Molly sighed. Talking with her brother Brian was one of the great pleasures in life. She kicked off her flats and put her feet on the desk. "What's goin' on?"

"You made the front page again. Sounds tense."

She grinned at Brian's simple statement. He never sugar-coated anything and always used as few words as possible.

"Tense is one way to describe it," she said, her eyes scanning the antacid wrappers that littered her desk.

"So you're living at work again," Brian concluded.

Molly knew what he was really saying. Her personal life was of constant concern to Brian, and although he never nagged, she knew her drinking bothered him immensely. He'd realized long ago that her happiness was measured in shot glasses, and when she was in a good place, she drank far less.

"So? Are you hangin' in there? How's your love life?"

She knew that if she didn't give him something, he'd hound her, and his girlfriend Lynne would try to set her up. Lynne meant well, but Molly believed there should be laws about hetero women trying to set up lesbians. She thought of Ari again for the tenth time that day. "Well," she said, "I did meet someone interesting."

"Really? Spill it."

"She's a witness in this case. She's the one who found the body."

"Geez," Brian exclaimed. "That must have been tough."

"Actually, she didn't seem that phased by it. She's a really strong person, and I think she's been through a lot." Brian chuckled. "Stop laughing," Molly commanded. "I know what that laugh means." Even as she said it, a smile was spreading across her face.

"So, go after her, sis. She sounds promising."

"No, nothing will happen," Molly concluded, using her standard line.

"Why?" Brian asked. He knew his sister and her King Kong-sized inferiority complex. Molly was the living definition of low self-esteem. He'd watched her grow up and be constantly harassed by all the kids at school. She'd always turned to him for a shoulder to cry on, always choosing to hold the anger and sadness in her heart rather than knock some heads around.

"Brian, she's gorgeous. And I mean like a model. She's not going to fall for a bull dyke with a badge."

"Again, *why not?*"

Molly shook her head. "Look, Bri, first, I don't even think she's gay. She's as much a femme as Lynne. And even if she is, beautiful lipstick lesbians don't go for women the size of tanks."

"You're probably right," Brian agreed. He knew that there was no arguing with Molly when she had already made up her mind. "So she's pretty, right?"

"Absolutely gorgeous."

"What color are her eyes?"

"Dark green."

"Does she have great legs?"

"They go on forever."

"Is she smart?"

"Yes."

"And how many times have you thought about her today?"

Molly opened her mouth and closed it. Brian was baiting her, but there was no point in lying to him. Even over the phone, she was totally transparent. No one else in her life knew her this well. That fact frustrated her and comforted her all at the same time.

"Call her," he said before he hung up.

She snapped the phone closed but didn't drop it back in her pocket. The Michael Thorndike file lay open on her desk, Ari's phone number conveniently handy. All Molly had to do was flip a few pages and press a few buttons on the phone. How hard was that? She'd just mustered her courage when she remembered their conversation that afternoon. It hadn't gone well. Molly had clearly crossed a line, and she suspected it had something to do with Ari's father. She'd hurt the woman, a fact that brought her more pain than the heartburn. She definitely wanted to apologize.

The phone was already ringing before Molly engaged her brain again. The voice that answered was soft and melodic.

"Hello, Ms. Adams. It's Molly Nelson." She bit her lip and held her breath. There was a long pause, which Ari obviously didn't feel obligated to fill. Molly gave a halfhearted laugh. "Well, at least you haven't hung up on me."

"Is there something I can do for you, detective?" The softness and melody were gone.

"I just wanted to say how sorry I was, you know, for saying what I did this afternoon, and bringing up your father. That was really out of line—" Molly closed her mouth to prevent further babbling. When Ari said nothing, Molly continued. "It's just this case . . ." She trailed off. "It's a career buster."

"And you're worried I'll screw it up," Ari said, completing her thought.

The detective swallowed hard. "Well, Ms. Adams, frankly, yes, I am."

"Why don't you call me Ari?"

"Okay," Molly replied, relief sweeping through her.

"Did you learn anything from your visit?"

"Not really," Molly sighed, almost grateful that someone was interested. Bouncing ideas off Andre was like hitting a wall of cotton. He just wasn't good at it. "I did determine that at least two of the partners are slimier than Thorndike. I'm surprised he was the one who was killed." Molly shifted her large frame in the chair. She'd been sitting in it for three hours reading reports and statements. Her ass was killing her. "What about you? Any luck?"

"Possibly."

"I thought you were shopping?" Molly teased.

Ari laughed and Molly joined her. "Okay, you caught me," she admitted.

"Well, tell me!" Molly exclaimed. "Solve this case for me, and I'll be yours for life." She sucked in her breath, amazed that the words had come from her mouth. She reached out to grab them, but they'd already sailed over the phone line.

"That's quite a proposition."

Molly nearly dropped the phone. Was Ari flirting with her? "Uh, well . . ."

"Don't worry, detective, I won't hold you to that." Ari relayed her suspicion about the pictures. "Hopefully, whatever it means will come to me. I know it's important."

Molly frowned, partly out of pride that she might have missed a clue, and partly at Ari's involvement. "You have to promise me something, Ari. If Bob Watson contacts you, promise me that you'll call."

"I haven't heard from him," she insisted adamantly.

"Just promise me. We've tailed Lily for the past two days and gotten zilch. The captain's calling off the detectives assigned to her. I'm convinced she doesn't know where he is, but somebody must. He has to have help. His picture is all over the news. Somebody would have seen him by now." Molly ran a hand through her curls and leaned back in her chair. "I'm sure he's called a friend. If he calls you—"

"I'll call you," Ari interjected. "I promise. Is there anything else, detective?"

Molly searched for a reason, any reason, to keep Ari on the line. She just loved the sound of her voice—so comforting and calm. After listening to men bark and belch and make other disgusting sounds all day, Ari's chuckle was welcomed. Unable to think of any pressing matter to discuss, she simply said, "Uh, no. I hope I didn't call too late. If I did, I'm sorry again."

"It's okay. I was just outside on my balcony."

Molly pictured Ari staring out into the city lights. "Sounds nice. I'm just finishing up work."

Ari took an audible breath. "If you're not too tired, why don't you join me? I could make us some tea and put on some jazz."

The offer hung in the air for a few brief seconds. Molly couldn't help but balk initially. It was her nature. "I'm not very presentable, and to be quite honest, I probably could use a shower."

Ari chuckled again. "I'll take my chances." Another awkward pause passed before she added, "I'd really like to see you."

Molly heard herself accept the invitation, perhaps a little too quickly, and was out the door with Ari's directions before she could change her mind.

Soft jazz seeped into the hallway and Molly hesitated. Why was she here? Absolutely exhausted, caught in the middle of an investigation, she *should* have been at home in her bed, yet here she was about to knock on a woman's door for some sort of pseudo-date at nine o'clock at night. The music reached a crescendo, nudging Molly forward.

At the sight of Ari, Molly knew she'd made the right decision. The business clothes had been shed in favor of shorts and a T-shirt, and Ari's long black hair fell freely over her shoulders and rested against her breasts.

"Come on in," Ari said, motioning to the couch as she headed back to the kitchen for the tea. Molly planted herself in the middle of the room and stared at the beautiful figure moving around the kitchen, reaching for cups, pulling her hair to one side and when she bent over . . .

Very uncomfortable and nervous, Molly tore her gaze away and studied the living room as if it were a crime scene.

The condo was immaculate, interior design touches every-where. What struck Molly the most was the sense of order.

Books were lined up on the shelves, tallest to shortest, the pillows situated on her sofa were perfectly positioned, and her CDs were organized by genre.

Famous prints adorned the walls, most notably Van Gogh's "Lilies." Molly wandered to the bookcase and squinted at the collection of framed snapshots. She instantly recognized one of Bob and Lily Watson, Ari smiling between them.

Next to it, a shiny silver frame caught her eye. Jack Adams with his arms around a beaming Ari in her Class C uniform, the day she graduated from the police academy. She studied the photo, comprehending the significance. Ari was a former cop. It explained her curiosity at the crime scene and possibly her relationship with her father. Ari wasn't a police officer now, so what did dad think of his daughter leaving the force?

"Surprised?" Ari asked, venturing from the kitchen with two mugs of tea. Molly nodded without comment. Tonight wasn't the time for family history.

Carrying both mugs, Ari led Molly outside. The detective admired the view and slowly took in the balcony's furnishings. The patio was as much a room in the house as any other. Rugs covered the cement, plants hung from the ceiling, and a small clay firepot sat in the corner.

"For those cold winter nights?" Molly joked.

"When I'm feeling especially rebellious toward my landlord, I burn a scented log."

They settled on the chaise lounges and sipped the tea. Complemented by a cinnamon stick and a sprig of mint, it tasted heavenly. The tea soothed her nerves or maybe it was the jazz humming softly in the background. She closed her eyes, and for the first time in days, felt her muscles relax. A heavy sigh escaped her lips.

"Do you want to talk about it?" Ari asked.

"I'm under an enormous amount of pressure with this case, and both the gun and the prime suspect are missing," Molly said, holding up a hand immediately, to stave off any apology from Ari. "I'm not trying to blame you for Watson's disappearance."

"I know you're not. Actually, I'm totally floored by Bob's behavior. Even I'm wondering about his innocence," Ari said softly. "At least, a little."

"That's ironic," Molly commented, sipping the tea. "I'm beginning to have some doubts of my own."

Ari's heart skipped a beat. "You mean you believe me?"

Molly shook her head. "I'm not sure what to believe. His name's on the wall, he doesn't have a good alibi, and he had multiple reasons to hate Thorndike, including an affair with his wife and a nearly destroyed business opportunity."

"But something's bothering you still," Ari concluded.

Molly nodded. "It's too easy. That usually doesn't happen with a smart killer, someone who doesn't leave prints and dumps the gun. I'm finding it a little hard to believe that he would leave Thorndike alive, at least long enough to write a dying declaration." She looked at Ari and pursed her lips, unable to admit out loud that she wondered if Bob had been set up.

"God, I hope that's true. I mean, I know running off made him look guilty, but I know Bob. I just can't believe he's capable of murder."

Molly heard the sincerity in her voice. "You're a loyal friend, aren't you?"

Tears welled in Ari's eyes. She looked into her mug and swirled the cinnamon stick, trying hard not to lose it. "Since high school. We dated briefly, but then we were just friends."

From the way Ari so succinctly explained their relationship, Molly knew there was much more. Jealousy swept over her. "Extremely close friends," she concluded.

"Yes, but just friends," Ari answered, sensing she needed to explain further. "Bob and I were never lovers. Our love is different."

"Because you owe him?" Molly asked, thinking back to the last thing Ari had said that afternoon: *Have you ever owed a debt you never thought you could repay?*

"Maybe," Ari said slowly, "this is my chance to pay him back." Ari hoped Molly realized the full implications of her sentence. She wouldn't back down, and she wouldn't stay out of the investigation, short of being arrested.

"Please be careful," Molly said.

Touched by the sentiment, Ari gently rested her hand over Molly's. When she made no effort to remove it, the detective's eyes widened at the sight.

"Is this all right?" Ari asked, smiling shyly. "You look a little shocked."

Her eyes still frozen to the spot, Molly answered, "I didn't think you held hands with women."

Ari smiled. "Well, I enjoy it, but it's been a while." She stroked Molly's large hands and long fingers. For a fleeting moment, she imagined them deep inside her.

Molly sat there, too petrified to return the gesture. Somehow, in the midst of a murder investigation, they had wound up together, looking at the stars and listening to jazz. Molly didn't have *planned* dates that went this well.

The chaise was so comfortable. She leaned back, concentrating on Ari's caress. Her hand was like silk and Molly imagined the rest of Ari's body would be just as smooth and soft.

She brought Ari's hand to her lips, kissing each fingertip lightly. Ari smiled, and that was all the encouragement Molly needed. She pulled Ari on top of her, and stared into her green eyes. Ari bent to kiss her mouth, but Molly shook her head no. "Not yet," she whispered. "I just want to touch you right now. I want to know every part of you." Molly reached underneath Ari's T-shirt and caressed her back, a sensation that gave Ari goose pimples. She wore no bra and her hardened nipples stood erect

59

against the fabric. Ari stared into Molly's twinkling eyes, made bluer by the moonlight. Her gaze fell to her chest and Molly's agile hands, moving slowly under the shirt, her thumbs teasing Ari's nipples. Ari moaned. Molly pushed Ari down on her back and let her hands slide down Ari's abdomen. She made slow circles around Ari's navel, her fingertips barely making contact with the cool flesh. Unable to stand anymore, Ari unbuttoned her shorts, but Molly clasped her hands together and brought them to her lips. "No." Ari gave Molly a look of frustration, but nodded. Molly's gaze wandered to Ari's calves. Like every other part of her body, her legs were muscular, and Molly took her time feeling each curve. She worked her way up to Ari's creamy white inner thighs, one of Molly's favorite parts of the female body. Here, she would not use her hands. She brought her lips to Ari's skin. Ari gasped as Molly's kisses drew closer to her center, and when the detective's tongue started working its way under her panties, she gasped.

Suddenly Molly blinked. "Did I fall asleep?"

"Only for a few minutes." Ari's eyes twinkled with amusement. "You must have been having some dream. You looked entirely satisfied."

Molly's face turned beet red. "God, I'm sorry," she said, standing up abruptly. "You invite me over and I'm snoring on your lounge." She shuffled her feet, not meeting Ari's gaze. "I should go." Ari tried to protest, but Molly's eyes were riveted to the front door, her exit from embarrassment. With her hand safely on the knob, she finally turned to Ari, expecting the beautiful woman to be angry or upset, but Ari simply touched her cheek.

"You need some rest," Ari whispered, her breath smelling of mint.

They were inches apart, Molly keenly aware of the electricity between them and unable to believe it was actually happening.

Ari caressed her face, and their foreheads touched. "I want to get to know you, Molly."

At the sound of her name, Molly became rooted to the carpet. Her hand dropped from the doorknob and she stood motionless, feeling much like a tree trunk. She closed her eyes, sensing Ari's kiss before she felt the soft lips against her own.

Chapter Seven
Tuesday, June 19
7:48 a.m.

"Fourteen, twelve," Jane announced as she served the ball into the left corner. It bobbed between the two walls and Ari managed to bounce it off the back glass before it struck the ground. They mercilessly pounded the racquetball, attempting winning shots, until Ari smashed one so low that it skidded across the hardwood. While she won the point, Jane won the game on the next serve, and proceeded to bellow a few bars of the *Rocky* theme and do a little victory dance.

Ari started to pack up, pretending to be disgusted by her antics. Jane would never win any good sportsmanship awards. They were equally matched and both hated to lose—only Ari didn't dance when she won. Dripping in sweat, they retreated to the locker rooms. Playing racquetball with Jane was a catch-22—

she hated exercising, but she loved the energetic high that followed a workout. If only there was a way to feel that good just from lying on her patio lounge chair.

Standing stark naked, Jane put her hands on her hips and confronted Ari. "Now, I want to know what's on your mind. That was the most apathetic racquetball game we've played in a long time. You weren't there and I want to know what you're thinking about. Is it Bob?"

At the mention of Bob's name, a wave of guilt came over Ari. She should have been thinking about Bob, but instead her thoughts were about Molly and their kiss, which apparently wasn't very good. She just shrugged her shoulders and prayed Jane would let it go. Half of the time Jane lost interest in a subject almost as quickly as it was mentioned, so Ari used the shoulder shrug on a regular basis.

"Well, I'm waiting. You know how much I like to win, but only if I feel it's a righteous victory."

Ari rolled her eyes. "God Jane, it was a racquetball game, not a civil rights march."

Making no effort to put on any clothes, Jane sat down on a nearby bench and stretched out. "If it's not Bob, then it's a woman." Ari didn't answer. She continued her methodical routine for dressing, working from toe to head. Jane actually liked watching Ari dress. Although she didn't want to date Ari, she certainly loved looking at her perfect body, and with Ari's dressing system, her breasts were almost always the last to be covered.

Ari pulled her shirt over her head and sighed. Jane was staring at her. Clearly, Jane wasn't losing interest. "Okay, the lead detective on Bob's case is totally hot, and we had a few unpleasant runins, and I think she kinda blames me for Bob running off, but I think she's attracted to me too. She's sort of threatened to arrest me if I don't stop interfering, but we made up. Anyway, she came over to my apartment last night and we kissed and then she just ran out the door without saying anything."

Jane sat there, her mouth open.

"Well?" Ari asked.

"I'm processing. Give me a moment."

Ari watched Jane formulate questions in her mind and reject each one. At one point, she started to open her mouth, and then she closed it. She knew that Ari hated to talk about her love life, so she needed to choose her questions carefully. Finally she smiled and asked, "What do you like about her?"

Ari sat down next to her friend and Jane saw she was blushing. "Everything. I mean I think she's gorgeous, but what really gets me is her personality."

Jane rolled her eyes. "Oh, God. That response means nothing. It's just the politically correct statement. What *specifically* do you like about her—and remember, you're talking to me. So if you're only attracted to her enormous breasts or her marvelous ass, that's okay."

Ari chuckled. "Well, I don't know her enough to say exactly. She was just impressive, yeah, I guess that's the word. And I felt like there was something between us immediately."

"Okay, don't quit your day job. It's apparent you're never going to be a novel writer because you suck at description."

"Look, I can't explain it, okay?" Ari shrilled.

"So she's a knockout?" Jane teased.

"Well, I think so, but I mean, she's not your stereotypical beauty."

"You mean like you."

"Right," Ari retorted. She grabbed her gym bag, avoiding Jane's gaze.

Jane knew the conversation was practically over. She rose and dressed quickly, not worrying about which item of clothing went on first.

"So, you kissed her and nothing happened," Jane summarized, slamming her locker shut.

"Well, I thought the kiss was great, but right after it was over she bolted out the door." Ari paused, remembering the look of panic on Molly's face. "Maybe I'm not her type," Ari concluded. "I kissed her and she just ran out. She didn't do anything."

"Did you? Did you try to stop her?"

Ari smirked. She hated it when Jane used logic, which occurred as often as a Halley's Comet sighting.

"As hard as it may be for you to believe this, Ari, you might have to be the aggressor. It's very possible she's intimidated by you." A few women strolled by in various states of undress. Jane's eyes followed a shapely brunette to the showers.

Ari shook her head. "Why would anyone be intimidated by me?"

Jane's head spun back to Ari. "You're kidding, right?"

"What are you talking about?"

"Ari, you're perfect. Perfect looking, perfect personality, perfect home, and you rarely do anything stupid." When Ari started to protest, Jane held up a hand. "Answer one question. Do you, or do you not, arrange your spices in alphabetical order?" Ari fidgeted. "I rest my case. You are totally anal, and everything you do is just so . . ." Jane searched for the word.

"Boring," Ari stated.

"No, that's not what I was going to say. You're just so *right*."

"I don't believe this." Ari hoisted her gym bag over her shoulder and walked toward the exit. The summer heat assaulted her the minute she opened the door. It was almost criminal to be this hot at nine in the morning, she thought.

Jane fell in step, choosing her words carefully. "Honey, it's nothing you do intentionally. It's just who you are, and the fact is, some people are uncomfortable."

"That is ridiculous," Ari argued with little enthusiasm.

Jane smiled smugly. She'd made her point. "Are you coming to the office today?"

"No, I'm going home to change, and then I thought I'd visit with Russ Swanson. I'll call you later," Ari said, closing the truck door.

However, her plans quickly changed when the secretary informed her that Mr. Swanson was with a detective. Ari could only imagine who that was, and she had every intention of staying out of Molly's way, at least in the professional sense. Most likely, she wouldn't have much luck romantically either. Molly had responded to Ari's pass with total disinterest, almost revulsion. Or had it been something else? Maybe she wasn't ready for a relationship, or Jane's theory might be correct, and Ari would have to take charge.

She checked her watch. It was nine o'clock, and the Speedy Copy would be open. If she couldn't speak with Russ Swanson, she'd talk to Kristen Duke, the person who saw Bob before Michael Thorndike's murder. Bob had said that he was training her for management, and since the Tempe store was the largest and most important in the chain, it was possible that he had checked in with her.

Ari headed for Tempe, Phoenix's neighboring college town and home to Arizona State University. The two cities were separated by the Salt River, a laughable name considering the puddle of water it usually contained. She crossed the historic Mill Avenue Bridge and puttered along the main drag, stopping at the eight traffic lights that lined the one mile stretch. Filled with coffee shops, boutiques and antique stores, many of which were still housed in the original brick buildings from the 1920s, Mill Avenue was the heart of Tempe. Historic clashed with nouveau, old timers melded with the punkers and the upper echelon endured the taunts of the street people.

Nestled between a Fifties-type diner and a hat shop, Speedy Copy enjoyed a prime location just across the street from the university. Obtaining the lease ten years ago was the smartest move Bob Watson ever made. Now it was his flagship store and accounted for over one-third of his total monthly business. Inside it was easy to see why he prospered. The store was filled with students, most of whom were feeding the self-serve machines with change. Ari could hear the money piling up.

At the counter a businessman in a blue pin-striped suit argued with a young woman whose name tag identified her as Kristen. The man suddenly stormed away, and Kristen shrugged her shoulders. She'd probably just seen her twenty-first birthday, dressed in tight black pants and a sheer black top that didn't cover her pierced belly button. Five studs lined each ear and her big doe eyes were heavily defined with black mascara. She was going for the goth look as evidenced by her two-toned hair, bleached blond except for the dark brown roots. For a split second Ari thought that she recognized Kristen from a fashion advertisement.

"May I help you?" she asked, her lips barely parting to form the words.

Ari pulled a flyer from her briefcase and set it on the counter. At the sight of the crime scene, Kristen balked. "What the hell? Are you a reporter?" She shoved the flyer back at Ari, color rising to her cheeks.

"No, I'm Bob's real estate agent, Ari Adams." Ari stuck her hand out and Kristen shook it, still rather suspicious. "I happened to be in the area, and I need some more of these made. Could you do that for me?" Ari held the flyer out, and Kristen took it reluctantly.

"How many do you need?" she asked, her eyes fixed on the paper.

"Well, hopefully only another hundred," Ari answered, trying to steer the conversation. "Now that we're past that terrible mess, I'm hoping it will sell quickly." Kristen scribbled instructions on a form, oblivious to Ari's attempt at conversation. She tried again. "Of course, Bob is the main suspect, and he's still missing."

Kristen's hand froze on the pad, and she met Ari's gaze with a worried look. "But Bob was with me, at least for part of the time." She stopped abruptly. "I mean, I told the police! Why are they still focusing on him?" Her voice carried, and at the mention of the word police, people started to stare.

"Hey, is there some place we could talk?" Ari asked gently, noticing that the counter was filling with customers ready to place orders or pay for their copies.

Kristen leaned toward a steroid-filled employee named Zeus and announced she was taking her break. Ari followed her to a nearby coffee bar in silence. Crowded with college students, it took another fifteen minutes to find an outside table and retrieve their order. After several hits of her mocha latte, Kristen said, "I can't believe they still suspect Bob. There is no way that he is capable of murder. He couldn't harm anyone. He's too nice a guy."

"Kristen, has he contacted you?"

She immediately shook her head. "The last time I saw Bob was Saturday night. We worked until eight thirty and then I went home to watch a movie with my roommate. You don't know how shocked I was to hear about all of this." She fished a cigarette and a match from her purse, her hands shaking as she brought it to her lips.

"How long have you worked for Bob?"

She struck the match on her shoe and lit her smoke. "About a year. Best damn job I've ever had and the only time a boss has ever treated me right." Ari noticed the brash demeanor returned immediately after a shot of nicotine. She stirred some creamer into her coffee, waiting for Kristen to continue. Kristen's sparkling green eyes bore down on her. "Why didn't you tell me you were Bob's friend when you came into the store?"

The question caught Ari off guard, and Kristen's eyes narrowed at her surprised reaction. Ari opted for a half-truth, not wanting to overplay her hand. She really had no business being here and questioning a material witness in the investigation, a fact Molly would quickly remind her of, if given the chance. "I didn't know you knew who I was," she said.

Kristen paused, assessing her response. She tapped the ash and glanced at her. "Bob's told me a lot about you. He said you used to date, back when you were straight."

"I didn't realize Bob made a habit of discussing my sexual preference with his employees," she retorted.

"It's no big deal, at least not with people my age. The whole gay thing is, like, totally cool." Ari smiled both at her optimism and her naïveté. "Not that I've tried it myself," she quickly added.

"So, why was Bob at the store on a Saturday night?" Ari asked.

"He's training me to be the manager. It's a big responsibility," she said with pride. "I've basically become Bob's right hand. I help him with lots of stuff and not just that one store. Maybe someday I'll be a vice president, or something." She sat up a little straighter at the notion.

"That's great," Ari said. "Let's talk about that night. Did Bob leave the store at any time? Did he go out?" She shook her head. "What about phone calls? Did anyone call him while you were there?" She shook her head again. "Did you notice anything unusual about his behavior during the evening, or did anything out of the ordinary happen?" Before she could automatically answer negatively, Ari reached out to touch her hand. "Kristen, listen to me, I know you've been asked these questions already, but I need you to really think. You may remember something that could help Bob."

At the mention of his name, she inhaled and leaned back. She sat still for a minute, taking several drags on her cigarette while Ari watched the smoke shroud her head. She tapped her finger on the plastic tabletop. "I do remember that Bob got a fax. I didn't see it because I was on the phone with this customer who was really stressed about leaving some important copying. I just remember looking over my shoulder and seeing Bob at the fax machine. Then I went back to my conversation with the guy."

"Did Bob seem upset?"

Kristen thought for a moment and shrugged. "Well, he started pacing and went back into the office. That's all I remember. I was really wrapped up with the guy on the phone. Kristen paused and took another drag. "Do you think that's important?"

"Probably not," Ari hedged. What bothered her, and what she wouldn't tell Kristen, was Bob's response to the fax. Pacing for Bob only meant one thing—he was agitated.

"What happened to the fax?"

She frowned. "By the time I got off the phone, he must have put it in his briefcase or shredded it, or whatever," she offered, the bored tone returning.

"Working at a copy shop must not be a really fun way to spend a Saturday night," Ari commented absently.

"It's cool," was Kristen's reply.

"You must be really devoted to your job. I mean, you're young and attractive, I would have thought you'd have a lot of dates on Saturday."

Her hesitation was brief and noticeable. She avoided Ari's gaze until the cigarette butt was squashed and swirled. "I've dated a lot of guys, but it wasn't until I got to college that I met a real man."

"I see. Did you ever meet Michael Thorndike? Did he ever come into the store?"

Kristen shook her head one last time, a blank expression on her face. She glanced at Ari's watch and stood up. "I've got to get back. I hope you can help Bob. He's a great guy." She left without saying good-bye and Ari was pretty sure she knew why.

Chapter Eight
Tuesday, June 19
8:32 a.m.

Morning traffic snaked down Central Avenue as every lawyer, CPA, government employee and corporate executive rushed, or rather inched, toward the beginning of the work day. The KPAZ news patrol confirmed what Molly knew: The pollution reading for the day was high. She sneezed again and reached in her jacket pocket for a tissue.

"Allergies?" Andre asked, his eyes on the road. Molly grunted, unable to talk or breathe at the moment. "I never had any," Andre continued, "until I moved here." He maneuvered the Chevy Cavalier into the parking garage for One Renaissance Square Tower.

"Yeah, well it's all you damn Midwesterners. Brought all your Bermuda grass and plants and pretty soon you can't tell this is a desert!" she snapped between blows.

"Hey, don't blame me, I'm from Philly!" Andre retorted. He pulled into a space by the elevators and turned to Molly. He was accustomed to her moods, and she could make Howard Stern cower in fear, but she was a damn good detective. He knew what the other guys said—half of them made jokes about her lesbianism and the other half wanted to bed her. For some reason, Captain Ruskin had targeted Molly for special abuse, assigning her to one messy case after another. As her partner, Andre endured his wrath by default, but he wouldn't transfer, not because of pride, but because Molly was teaching him more about police work than anyone else ever had. The Michael Thorndike case was wearing him down, but it was killing Molly. She was pulling double shifts, and judging from her appearance, she wasn't sleeping well. Andre had also heard rumors from other gay officers that Molly was drinking excessively at the bars. He watched as she took a deep breath, clearing her sinuses.

"Okay, let's go," she said.

For the second time in as many days, they took the elevator to the fifth floor, home of the Speedy Copy corporate offices. On their previous visit, they had waved their search warrant and rummaged through Bob Watson's office, finding very little except voluminous files that would take days to comprehend. Molly wanted a second pass while they waited for their scheduled interview with Russ Swanson, a man who seemed busier than the president and almost as unreachable.

No one said a word as they headed for Bob's corner office, but everyone's eyes looked up, having witnessed the spectacle from the day before when Bob Watson lost his right to privacy. Yesterday Russ Swanson had not been in, his door closed, but today it was open, Swanson bending over his desk, talking into a phone headset and writing on a tablet. She motioned Andre to start searching Bob's office again, while she stopped in the doorway and eavesdropped.

Russ gave a slight laugh before interrupting. "Look, let's get this straight, we both have needs that must be met . . . yeah, I'm sure we can work together . . ." He listened and grunted affirmatively, doodling on his writing tablet. "No one is talking about anything illegal, Kent," he interjected, "the law is on our side. Well, you think about it. I know you're a smart businessman, and you'll do the right thing . . . Okay, 'bye."

Molly knocked on the open door and stepped into his office just as he was dialing another number. "Mr. Swanson, I'm Detective Nelson. I believe we have an appointment?" Swanson reluctantly removed his headset and came around the desk. The man who shook her hand was handsome and tall, possessing a strong jaw and angular face with a trimmed goatee that created a professorial look. Only his long blond hair pulled back into a tight ponytail clashed with the rest of the Brooks Brothers image.

"Detective, thank you for accommodating my schedule. I'm sure you're very busy and I want to assist you and Robert in any way I can." Molly instantly noticed the change in his tone. He was working for sincere, but it came out condescending. "Please sit down. If you don't mind, I just need to speak with my secretary for a moment, and I'll be right back." He flashed a smile that matched the tone and hurried out, providing Molly with an opportunity to survey his office.

The floor plan was an exact duplicate of Watson's office, but the similarities ended there. One of the challenges during the initial search had been Watson's lack of organization. Papers littered his desk haphazardly, some covered with coffee stains, piles of folders and samples were scattered around the room, and while it was certainly convenient for the search, it bothered Molly that his only file cabinet had been unlocked, one of the drawers open. Security and neatness were not his strengths, two qualities that she naturally associated with methodical murderers. If anyone was methodical, it was Russ Swanson. She'd noticed a keypad entry on his office door, perhaps to protect the

73

glass cases full of antiques that lined the walls. Watson's office had no similar technology and hadn't been locked at all. Swanson's desk was immaculate, free of clutter, with two phone messages centered on his blotter. Molly stood and stretched, letting her eyes fall to the desk, one from Lily Watson and the other from Cyril Lemond—*how interesting*.

A minute later, Swanson breezed back in, closing the door behind him. He glanced at his watch as he lowered himself into his chair. "So sorry to keep you waiting, Detective. Now, how can I help?"

"First, Mr. Swanson, I need to know if you've been in contact with Bob Watson in the last seventy-two hours."

"No, I have not," he answered, pursing his lips. "The last time I spoke with Robert was Saturday morning. Actually, if you asked the secretary, she would probably call it a fight, considering most of the building probably heard us."

Molly quickly noted that Swanson was the first person to call him "Robert." "What was the problem, if you don't mind discussing it?"

Swanson tugged at the cuffs of his expensive dress shirt. Molly added the word fastidious to her notes. "Robert and I tended to argue about the same things constantly," he said, as if reading a prepared speech. "It all comes down to the fact that I'm more aggressive than he is, more of a risk taker."

Thinking of his previous telephone conversation, Molly thought to ask, "Does that include breaking the law?"

He cracked a smile. "Of course not, Detective."

"What about bending the law to suit your purposes?"

Swanson leaned back in his chair, craning his neck. "That's a gray area. I'm a businessman, and my goal is to make a lot of money. I'm also a pragmatist. I know that some laws actually hinder progress. So in answer to your question, yes, sometimes I must interpret what the laws say and make a judgment call."

"So you've never done anything illegal to close a deal?" Molly asked.

"If a tree falls in the forest and no one hears it, does it really make a sound?" Swanson replied.

Molly's blood boiled. She heard this type of rationalization from killers and rapists all the time. Everybody made an excuse to justify themselves. In her mind, right was right and wrong was wrong. She didn't see much difference between Russ Swanson and the murderer she'd put away last month. "So the end justifies the means, right?" she summarized, swallowing her true opinion.

Swanson nodded slowly. "I suppose you could put it like that. Of course, Robert didn't agree with me. He's a Boy Scout when it comes to business, and he knows it. That's why he hired me in the first place. He has the instincts, but he needed me to close the deals."

"And that's what you did with the downtown store?"

"Exactly," Swanson said, his eyes twinkling. "That never would have happened if it was left to Robert, regardless of the previous unpleasantness between the two of them." Molly assumed his euphemism referred to Thorndike's affair with Lily. "I made that deal work," he said, pointing at his chest, "and I'm damn proud of it."

Molly didn't bother to add that editorial comment to her notes. "Mr. Swanson, where were you last Saturday night?"

For the first time, his face paled, and the smile that seemed permanently transfixed on his face wavered. "I was with a friend," he answered guardedly. "A male friend, Detective."

Molly didn't look up from her notes. She knew what he meant. "And his name?"

A deep sigh escaped from Swanson's lips and he closed his eyes. "I assume it is absolutely necessary for me to give you that piece of information? To remove suspicion from myself?"

"That's correct," Molly said.

His eyes opened and he reached for his Mont Blanc fountain pen and a scratch paper, carefully unscrewing the lid. He wrote quickly and handed the result to Molly. As the name registered, she understood why Russ Swanson was hesitant to say it out loud. Not many men could claim to be sleeping with a superior court judge, one who was supposedly happily married to the mayor's daughter.

She took a few seconds to gather her thoughts, becoming more uncomfortable by the minute. Russ Swanson had just described his partner as a Boy Scout, and someone with scrupulous standards. Could a Boy Scout murder someone in cold blood? Doubts were clouding her mind as she found herself *liking* Bob Watson.

Swanson glanced at his watch, but Molly pretended not to notice. She thumbed through her notes, her mind cross-connecting all of the other information. Molly was at her best during interviews, and she prided herself on her thoroughness. "Mr. Swanson, I've noticed as we've talked that you have always referred to Bob Watson as Robert. Why is that? Everyone else calls him Bob."

"Yes, *Bob*," Swanson repeated with sarcasm. "I'm sorry, but I believe your name is a part of your professionalism. Robert sounds much more businesslike than *Bob*. Given the choice between the two, I'll stick with Robert."

Molly nodded and closed her notebook as the door swung open. Andre rushed to Molly and leaned over her shoulder, ignoring the surprised look from Russ Swanson. "I may have found the gun," he whispered.

Chapter Nine
Tuesday, June 19
12:04 p.m.

If questioned later, Ari would have to admit she didn't remember much of the drive back from Tempe, her mind accepting an uncomfortable realization—Bob was having an affair with Kristen Duke. *She hadn't met a real man until she went to college.* Bob was most likely that man and Ari really wasn't surprised. He had always attracted women.

She debated whether to tell Molly. It was just like the picture of Michael Thorndike—both gave Ari a nagging feeling like a guest who wouldn't leave. There was nothing concrete, and there was no way she would complicate Molly's life further, not after she'd already triggered Bob's disappearance. She decided to wait until she could give the detective something solid.

She found herself sitting in the visitor's parking lot of the police station. She'd just driven here on instinct, Jane's words nagging in her brain. Although she wanted to help Bob, she had to see Molly. She had to know the detective's feelings.

The lot was crowded, and Ari took the last available spot, right across from the front door. She hadn't been to police head-quarters in over three years, and then only briefly to deliver her mother's funeral information to her father. He had refused to make the arrangements, declaring that since he and Ari's mother were divorced, it was Ari's responsibility to plan the service. It had been the most gut-wrenching time of her life. The death of her mother combined with the abandonment of her father had left her totally alone.

Now she suddenly dreaded going inside. Several uniformed and plainclothes officers wandered in and out, and Ari was certain she recognized some of them. Finding her cell phone and Molly's number, she let the wonders of technology carry her to the third floor where the police detectives worked.

"Nelson."

"Molly, are you busy?"

Clearly surprised, Molly sputtered, "Uh, well, yes."

Ari could hear voices in the background, one of whom she remembered from the past. "Is that Captain Ruskin I hear squawking?"

"That would be correct," Molly said. "Is there something I can do for you?"

"I'm in the parking lot. Could you take a bathroom break and come down here? I need to speak to you, and I'm really not up for meeting and greeting all of my dad's old cronies." The line went silent, and Ari could hear Molly answering a question for someone else before returning to the conversation.

"That would be fine. Thank you for calling," she said before hanging up.

Two minutes later Molly poured herself into the SUV and shut the door. She put her head against the seat and stared at Ari with tired eyes. Ari took Molly's hand in her own, very aware of the bustling activity outside. "Bad day?" she whispered.

"Bad case," Molly responded. She held the moment for as long as she could, savoring the cool touch of Ari's palm. Upstairs, David Ruskin was reaming Andre for not finding the gun the day before, when they had initially searched Watson's office. Of course, Ruskin blamed Molly. *She* wasn't the rookie. *She* should have checked the filing cabinet more thoroughly. Molly debated mentioning it to Ari, but decided to let it go until the results were back. No need to worry her unnecessarily. "You said you wanted to talk?"

Ari sat up straight. "Actually, Detective, I'm rather upset with you." Molly's face filled with concern. "In all of my years of dating, I've never had someone run away from me. I've been turned down and in one case, a woman screamed at me and slammed the door, but you're the first person to bolt out of my apartment like it was on fire."

Molly looked down, her face coloring. "I'm sorry about that. I was embarrassed, kind of like right now. I mean, it's not like I've never been kissed by a woman, but never anyone like you. No one as beautiful . . ." Her voice fell off, and the words hung at the edge of the emotional cliff. She decided to take the leap. She looked at Ari and said, "I'm not the kind of woman who gets phone calls from gorgeous women."

Ari hated it when Jane was right. She squeezed the detective's hand and brought it to her lips. "Make no mistake about how attractive I think you are," Ari said.

Molly studied Ari. She couldn't believe this was happening. Her screaming captain seemed ten thousand miles away while she was on some secluded island with this beautiful woman who tenderly kissed her big knuckles.

"As much as I'm enjoying this," Molly murmured, "I have to get back to work. Will you go out with me tomorrow night? I promise I'll stay through the whole date."

Ari smiled and leaned toward Molly for a kiss when laughter erupted in front of them. Ari turned and saw three large cops exiting the precinct, their eyes focused on Ari's windshield.

She blushed and Molly nodded in understanding. This wasn't the place for romance, and if Captain Ruskin walked out that door, she would be a beat cop again in a second. Her hand still clasped in Ari's, she asked, "Is Ari short for anything?"

"Aria."

"How appropriate," she whispered.

The feel of Molly's caress stayed with Ari all the way to her office. Her passion and lust, if she would admit it, lay buried deep in her heart, a muscle that had experienced no use, except in the medical sense, for a long time. Although her relationship with Trina had ended a year ago, the proverbial fire had smothered a year before that, but they were both too stubborn to break up. At least one out of their two years together had been good. Ari consoled herself with a fifty percent figure. If that were lottery odds, it'd be great.

Now, Ari's emotions were getting a workout. Dating someone was not in the prescribed game plan. A methodical planner, Ari did not envision becoming involved for at least another eight months, thus allowing herself time to finish her broker's courses and possibly start her own company. At that point, love could be penciled into her calendar, once her professional life was in order. Molly was not on the agenda, not to kiss and certainly not to date, but if her cell phone rang right at that moment, and Molly asked to meet at the Hyatt for an afternoon tryst, Ari would shatter the speed limit to get there.

Analyzing her feelings drained her energy, and for now, her mind needed to focus on work, which proved all consuming once she got to the office. A telephone remained glued to her ear for the next two hours. She followed up on loans for her buyers, called potential buyers for her listings, haggled with an agent over an offer, gave an ultimatum to a difficult client ("Clean up your house or I'm canceling the listing") and threatened some hostile renters with a lawsuit if they didn't allow her listing to be shown.

At two o'clock Ari scooped up her papers and trudged toward the conference room. As she entered, her boss was starting one of his tasteless jokes. "What do a blond and a screen door have in common? The more you bang it, the looser it gets." She took her seat and listened to Harry Lewis's booming laugh, clearly amused by his own sense of humor. Ari noticed the two other associate brokers laughed along, both of them spineless plebes who were afraid of Harry Lewis's power.

"Harry, are we having a meeting?" Ari asked pointedly.

His capped teeth smiled at her and Ari seethed. He was a total ass, a slimeball underneath his thousand-dollar suit and gold pinky ring. He steepled his fingers against the wide expanse of his chest and said, "Sorry, Ari, we were just letting off a little male steam," he said, obviously not sorry at all.

She had never thought she was capable of hate, but she gritted her teeth at this despicable man with his pasty face and three chins that folded over the knot of his tie, reflections of the gluttonous lifestyle he enjoyed. The two other associate brokers shuffled papers and pretended to take notes, trying to make themselves as small as possible. Ari was sure they wanted to crawl under the conference table.

She had shrugged off Harry's advances and jokes since joining Allstar, which only increased his arousal. Realizing he wasn't getting anywhere, he promoted her to associate broker, no doubt thinking it might improve his chances to get in her pants. He was sure all lesbians secretly desired a man, and in her case, he could make her switch teams.

She quietly seethed while he quickly started the meeting. She focused on the business at hand, but within five minutes her mind had drifted from real estate to Michael Thorndike's death and the little niggling feelings that kept tickling the back of her mind. There was something about that wall . . .

"Don't you agree, Ari?" Harry bellowed.

Ari jumped from her trance and glared at him. "Whatever you say, Harry."

"Oh, really?" he grinned. "You want to get naked with me right now?" Her face went crimson. Making a rare split-second decision, she rose, gathered her papers, and left. In two minutes she had all of her personal belongings in a small box and she headed for the front door. The three men remained in the conference room and watched her through the glass as she stopped at the reception desk and hit the intercom button. "Attention Allstar agents: this announcement is to inform you that as of this moment, I quit." A sharp moan swelled in the room. "And," she continued, "it is also to let you know that Harry Lewis can be seen every Friday night at the 307 Club's weekend drag show. He goes by the name Florida Orange. Thank you."

Ari watched Harry leap from his chair, his huge belly catching the front of the table and sending him to the floor. She whisked out of the office laughing the whole way. It would have been nice if Jane had been there, since she was the one who'd told Ari about Harry's double life.

For a moment, Ari panicked. She had made three unplanned decisions in her whole life: the first one she never spoke of, the second was to become a real estate agent and now, she'd just quit—no notice, no backup offer, nothing. She searched her emotions for an ounce of regret, but all she felt was relief. Money was certainly not a problem. Her financial portfolio was exceptional. She had worked diligently over the last ten years, too diligently, according to Trina. Ari had begged to differ, arguing that a relationship should not be all consuming. Since neither of them was willing to walk across the great divide and sacrifice anything, they broke up.

As she cruised down Seventh Street, it occurred to her that Bob's corporate office was a mile away. It might be a good time to drop in on Russ Swanson and use the element of surprise to her advantage. She punched in the number and was tersely informed that Mr. Swanson had left for the day.

Sitting in the SUV, she wasn't sure what to do next. Officially unemployed, there were plenty of things she could be doing, such as notifying her clients and finding another place to hang her license, but instead, she flipped open her cell phone and called Lily.

"Oh, Ari, have you heard from Bob?" she asked expectantly.

"I'm sorry, Lily, I haven't heard a word. I'm sure he'll call eventually," Ari added, not really sure of anything anymore when it came to understanding her friends. "Besides checking in with you, I called because I have some clients who are interested in joining a club, and I'm not exactly sure which one to recommend. You like yours, don't you?"

"Absolutely!" Lily gushed. "Your clients would love The Desert Racquet Club, and I'd be more than happy to give them a tour, just tell me when."

That was the name she couldn't remember. "Thanks, Lily. Let me run it by them, and I'll let you know."

"No problem," Lily said, signing off.

Ari raced home for her tennis whites. She'd gladly given up tennis for racquetball when she saw how much smaller the court was. Hopefully, there wouldn't be a need to embarrass herself today.

Getting past the club's front lobby proved easier than she thought. The clerk was obviously family, and very understanding about Ari's predicament. She was here as a guest of Deborah Thorndike, but "Debs" had forgotten to notify the desk, and Ari didn't know where to find her.

The young woman glanced at her watch. "That's easy," she said in a husky voice. "She's in the sauna, every day from three to

83

four." The clock above the desk read three fifteen, and although Ari did not relish interviewing someone in the nude, it was unavoidable. She thanked the baby dyke for her help and followed the corridor to the changing rooms.

By three twenty-five, she was melting on a wooden bench with two other women who were engaged in small talk. She listened, hoping one of them would mention a clue as to her identity. Ten minutes later, just as Ari was about to give up, the older woman rose and said, "See you tomorrow, D," before leaving.

Ari took a long look at the woman next to her. A fluffy white towel covered her midsection and she wore a second one as a turban. She was slight and petite, her feet barely touching the tile floor. Sensing Ari's presence, she turned her head and Ari saw a face worthy of a painting. Deborah Thorndike could be described as flawless, complete with full lips and a Romanesque nose, but her most beautiful feature was her eyes, large and brown. As she adjusted her body towel, her hands seemed to float back to her sides.

Now that eye contact had been established, Ari decided to get right to it. She hated saunas and looking at this woman was making her light-headed. "Hello," she began.

"Hello." The word hung in the air, and like everything else about Deborah Thorndike, it seemed to glide away. "I haven't seen you here before. You must be new."

"Actually I am. Just moved from Oregon."

"Lovely place," Deborah remarked. "My husband and I used to have a summer home there." Ari couldn't help but notice there was a slight catch in her voice.

"Oh, you don't have the home anymore?"

When she spoke, Deborah's tone was even. "No, I don't have the husband."

"I'm sorry. Was this long ago?"

"Actually only a few days."

"You're doing remarkably well. I mean, to be back here at the club so soon."

"It's really the only enjoyment I've ever had. I think my husband was terribly jealous of the time I spent here. I'm a very good tennis player, and every time I won a tournament, he rewarded me by taking another mistress. His way of getting even." Just as her tone remained neutral, so did her body. Her face betrayed not a hint of emotion and her hands remained in her lap. It was as if she were reporting the evening news. Ari found the effect chilling. "I'm sorry, I don't know why I'm boring you with this," she said, her face becoming animated for a moment.

"Oh, I don't mind. Sometimes it helps to talk to a stranger."

Deborah looked around. "You must be right. I've said more to you in the past two minutes than I have to my shrink, my mother or my best friend in the last few days." At this they exchanged smiles.

"Actually, I know a little of what you're going through. My husband left me for another woman," Ari lied.

"Then you know what it's like. All the lame excuses, the credit card receipts that he just can't explain, the women who call and hang up." She threw her head back and laughed. "God, men are so transparent!"

"Then of course," Ari pressed, "there's always one that falls in love with him."

Deborah stared at her, the emotion immediately evaporating again.

"I'm sorry. Did I say something wrong?"

Deborah's gaze was steady. "You really do know, don't you?"

Ari nodded sympathetically. She understood exactly how Deborah felt. It didn't have anything to do with a husband, but everything to do with Trina, the last woman she had let—or *would* ever let—live with her.

The towel covering Deborah's body slid to her waist, revealing small, round breasts. Deborah didn't seem to care as she crossed her legs and stretched. "He said he met her during a business transaction, but you never know. It could have been at a bar or a friend could have set them up." She raised an eyebrow. "That really happened one time. One of our closest friends found him a girlfriend. Amazing, huh?" Ari just shook her head, since, at the moment, she was in no position to judge anyone else's deception. "Anyway, at first it started like all the others, and I figured it would end like all the others, but it didn't. I noticed Michael was changing, his moods, his attitude. Usually when he had a bimbo, he was extra attentive to me when he was at home. That's how I knew he was fooling around again." She paused and took a deep breath. The steam was getting to both of them. "This time, he withdrew from me entirely. That's why it took me twice as long to figure out he was cheating again, because he wasn't behaving any differently, or so I thought. Actually, he'd fallen in love with this woman."

"Was it mutual?" Ari croaked, gasping from the steam.

"Oh, yes. This woman had been calling for weeks talking about business or charity work that she needed to discuss with Michael. Business, my ass," Deborah retorted.

Ari's mind was racing. She had so many questions, but she had to remain cool and detached, and she couldn't forget she was playing straight. "So, how did you find out?"

There was a long pause. Deborah cocked her head at an angle and spoke very slowly. "I was reading in bed, and it was exactly ten thirty-eight. Michael appeared in the doorway, smelling of her perfume, and announced, 'We're getting divorced.' Then he walked to the closet, pulled out a bag, threw some clothes into it, and went into his study."

"What did you do?"

"I went to the door and listened. He was talking to this woman, telling her he'd officially left me, and then they made a

86

plan to meet later that night." She stopped and looked down for a moment, breaking the rhythm of her story. Her cheeks reddened. "I couldn't let him go, do you understand that? If he walked out that door, I knew he'd never be back. I'd never have an opportunity to convince him to stay. We'd never have another chance. I knew I couldn't let him leave, so I went into the kitchen, found a butcher knife and slashed the tires of both of our cars."

"You did what?"

Instead of repeating herself, Deborah explained her position. "I couldn't let him leave, and I knew there was no way his little sex kitten would show her face after she heard what I'd done."

"He could have called a cab," Ari reasoned. Despite the beads of sweat that were pouring down her face, she still saw the blush.

"I also pulled the phone cords out of the wall and threw our cell phones in the pool."

"Jesus," Ari mumbled under her breath. "Did he stay?"

Deborah turned away, adjusted her towel properly and replaced her hands by her side. "No," she whispered.

"How long ago was this before he died?"

"A few weeks," Deborah said softly.

Ari sensed the conversation was over and made a move to leave the sauna. "Did you tell the police this information when they questioned you about his murder?"

Deborah's head tilted up and her eyes narrowed. "I never said my husband was murdered."

"Um, well . . ." Ari stumbled over her words, trying to recover. "Yes, you did."

"I did not," Deborah insisted, her anger showing. "Who the hell are you?"

There was no way the truth would help. "I'm a reporter with *New Times*. I was just trying to get a story."

Deborah sprang up, her towel falling to the floor. She grabbed the poker that rested near the coals and placed it inches from Ari's face. "If you ever come near me again, I won't just slash your *tires*."

Ari put her hands up in surrender. "It's okay, I'm going." Deborah's eyes were wild, and she waved the poker back and forth, the heat from the tip radiating against Ari's face. "Really, please, think about what you're doing. I'm going." Ari took a step back toward the door, moving slowly, very aware of the poker's glowing end, just inches from her face. Deborah held her ground, debating what to do.

At that moment, the sauna door opened and two puzzled women stepped through the steam. Ari turned and ran immediately. She changed in one of the toilet stalls, and when she was absolutely sure Deborah Thorndike was nowhere to be found, she raced through the lobby, totally ignoring the baby dyke calling good-bye.

Chapter Ten
Tuesday, June 19
8:00 p.m.

Jane worked her way through the Smiley's crowd, amazed that the nightspot was so crowded on a Tuesday night. The place was packed, and people were shoulder to shoulder. Techno dance music echoed throughout the bar and restaurant, eliminating the possibility of meaningful conversation. The bar area was separated from the restaurant by a simple step, and by ten o'clock the drinkers seeped into the dining area making the division indistinguishable. Most of the patrons didn't care, and new friendships and relationships blossomed when total strangers asked to share a chair, or if they were really trashed, a meal.

When Jane found Ari sitting alone at a table, she'd already downed three whiskey sours and was thinking of a fourth.

"One, two, three," Jane counted deliberately, her newly manicured index finger pointing at each glass. "For someone who is a nondrinker, you're giving alcoholics a bad name. Why are you drinking?" Jane shouted, attempting to raise her voice over the music.

"I'm calming my nerves," Ari stated.

"What?" Jane shouted, turning her ear to Ari. When she still couldn't hear Ari's response, Jane led Ari to the back room, out of the crowd and away from the music.

"My day was a bit over the top, even for me," Ari said, as they climbed on to two barstools.

"Well, I found out Bob was having an affair with one of his employees, at least I'm pretty sure. You were right about Molly, and I'm having a date with her tomorrow night, I quit my job, and then to complete the afternoon, I faked my way into the Desert Racquet Club to interview Deborah Thorndike, got a really good look at her beautiful breasts in the sauna, found out that she was rather possessive of her husband, and that she's somewhat psychotic."

"Excuse me?"

"I made a mistake, and she realized I was a phony. She threatened me with a hot poker. For a moment, I thought she might burn out my eye."

Jane's mouth dropped open. Then she quickly recovered. "I'd say you had a full day," she commented. "Reserving the right to discuss the affair and the date later, I think I'll start with the psycho. So do you think this Deborah could have killed her husband?"

"Most definitely," Ari said sarcastically. "I think this woman could be a hired assassin if she wanted to. She's not someone you want to have pissed off at you. And since Thorndike made it a hobby of pissing her off by fooling around, I'd say she just moved into the prime suspect spot. Get this, he was going to leave her for another woman."

"No shit! Was it Lily?"

"I'm not sure. Supposedly that was over, but if Bob was having an affair and Lily knew, then maybe they started up again. And Deborah said something about charity work so I'm not sure," Ari concluded.

"Did you tell Molly about this woman?"

"Not yet. Besides, as Thorndike's wife, I'm sure the police have already questioned her," Ari said, rationalizing her reluctance to recount the sauna story to Molly.

"Yeah, but I'll bet none of them nearly got skewered in the process," Jane added, already reading Ari's hesitation. "That woman is dangerous, Ari."

Ari nodded in agreement and drained her fourth whiskey sour. She motioned for the bartender, but Jane dismissed him with a wave.

"What!" Ari bellowed, the alcohol definitely taking over her. "I'm fine. I can drink at least one more."

"Only if that bartender wants to lose his left nut. You've had enough."

Ari opened her mouth and closed it again. Jane was right, and her head was starting to pound.

"Now I want the good stuff. Tell me about your upcoming date. Do you think you'll have sex?"

Ari giggled. She felt like a teenager, getting a chance to have a high school experience that she'd never known. Never once had she sat on the phone and gossiped with another girl about a romance. Girls certainly didn't talk with girls about *girls*. "I thought about what you said, about me needing to take the lead. And, I went downtown and met her in the parking lot of the police station."

"And?"

"And I was going to kiss her, but there were too many people around. We held hands and gazed into each other's eyes."

Jane laughed at the dopey expression on Ari's face. She wished she had a video camera, because Ari wouldn't believe how she was acting after the alcohol wore off.

"And did she seem interested or did she want to run away?"

Ari shook her head. "Oh, no. She was totally into it, and she looked so hot."

"I need a drink and a woman," Jane announced, motioning the bartender and scanning the room for interesting prospects. "No more living through your love life."

After three espressos for Ari and two gin and tonics for Jane, they headed to the door. Suddenly Jane grabbed Ari's arm and propelled her outside toward a middle-aged blond man heading for a Buick.

"Russ," Jane called. He spun around, a surprised and confused expression on his face.

As they reached the car, somewhat panting from the sprint, Jane stuck out her hand, which Russ shook while she provided an explanation. "Hi, it's me—Janey? We met a few weeks ago here at the wine tasting?"

It took Russ Swanson a few seconds, but a look of recognition crossed his face. "Oh, well, hello, Jane. It's nice to see you again." He was what Ari thought of as a typical gay man, someone who could set off gaydar whether he was at the Pride festival or a church.

Jane edged her way between Russ and his car. "You know Ari Adams, right?"

Ari smiled, hoping the alcohol on her breath wasn't too obvious. "We've met at Bob's parties several times," Ari said. Russ nodded his agreement.

"We're wondering if you could answer a few questions," Jane pressed. "You see, Ari's been looking into the murder of Michael Thorndike."

At the mention of Thorndike's name, Russ Swanson's face fell. He stepped around Jane and jammed his key into the lock. "I have absolutely nothing else to say about Michael Thorndike or Robert Watson. Good night ladies." He quickly got into his car and turned over the ignition.

"But Russ," Jane pleaded over the engine's roar. He threw the Buick into reverse, and if Ari hadn't pulled Jane away, she probably would have lost some toes. They watched Russ speed out of the parking lot. "I'll bet he's hiding something," Jane ventured, tapping her chin with her index finger.

"Really, Sherlock? You think so?" Ari said sarcastically, heading for the truck.

"Oh no," Jane said, grabbing Ari's keys from her hand. "You're not driving."

"I'm fine now, Jane."

"That's what all drunk drivers say." They reached the SUV and Jane stood at the back, her hands on her hips, shaking her head. "Would you look at that? I hate it when people do that." She pointed at the position of a small Ford compact parked next to the SUV, hugging the striped line, blocking the passenger door from opening. "You'll never be able to get in. I'll have to back out first." Ari watched Jane slide into the driver's seat and put the SUV in reverse. Something was clicking in her mind, like a piece of flint ready to catch. The idea was close, but it wasn't ready to come.

She got in and Jane started to prattle about real estate. Ari didn't hear much; she was too busy trying to bring the brainstorm to the front. It had something to do with the wall behind the bar. She needed to see it again.

"Jane, turn here," Ari pointed.

"Where are we going?" Jane asked.

"I need to make a stop," Ari said evasively. After several more lefts and rights, Jane realized they were going toward the Watson house. "Oh no, I'm not going into any crime scene with you. No way."

When they pulled up to the curb, the house looked a little

ominous in the dark, and Ari noticed the crime scene tape had been recently removed.

"Ari, I'm not going in there," Jane insisted.

"You don't have to. Just wait here. I'll only be a minute." Ari grabbed a small flashlight from the glove compartment and left the truck, while Jane accused her of being a moron.

Ari glanced up and down the street. Lights were on in most of the houses, and most everyone was home, providing her with a sense of security, however hollow it might be. She left the front door open and stepped into the living room. A stale smell flooded her nostrils, and she made a mental note to buy some air fresheners. Obviously the body was gone, but a wave of relief swept through her anyway as she stared at the spot. Now it was just a patch of caked brown.

She hesitated before advancing, listening intently for any strange noises. Shadows danced all over the walls, and total darkness loomed beyond the circle of her flashlight. She walked behind the bar and crouched. Like the floor, the bloody letters were more brown than crimson, the strokes uneven and ghastly. She realized the name *Robert* was written at an angle, tilting upward. The capital *R* was close to the baseboard, and then the letters ascended, the *T* almost two feet off the ground. She imagined Michael Thorndike, shot twice, twisting in the tiny space to write a final message, every movement extracting what little life was left in him. She studied the letters again, tracing them in the air with her finger.

And the answer clicked, just like her dad always said it would. At that exact moment, she realized that she wasn't alone. She turned her head a fraction of an inch before everything went black.

Chapter Eleven
Tuesday, June 19
9:06 p.m.

The explosion in her brain came with consciousness. She didn't want to open her eyes. There were voices whispering, but it felt better to stay still. Her throat was totally dry, her tongue a shriveled raisin.

The voices grew louder, and she recognized one as Jane's. "Ari, Ari, open your eyes!" She tried to focus on Jane's panicked face but found herself staring at Molly Nelson.

"Ari, come on now," Molly coaxed. Her head was pounding, but she finally blinked. It hurt like hell. They had moved her out to the patio and laid her on the only remaining piece of furniture, a lounger. Molly and Jane hovered over her, but she saw several uniformed officers standing nearby. Again, the elder Watson's house was a crime scene.

"Set her up a bit more, Jane," Molly instructed. The two women pulled her into a sitting position, which released several more bombs in her head. "That's going to hurt for a while. You've got quite a bump back here," Molly said, gently rubbing the crown of her head.

"Is she going to be all right? She looks totally out of it."

Molly stared into her eyes. "Well, she should be checked out by a doctor, but I'd say she just got a good knock." She handed Ari a bottle of water, which she drank greedily. "Can you tell me what happened?"

Even in her semiconscious condition, Ari knew better than to tell the whole truth. "I wanted to check on the house. I bent down to look at the wall. Someone knocked me out while my back was turned."

"Jesus, Ari," Jane gasped, "you could have been killed! I told you to stay out of this."

"So did I," Molly interjected. "Let's not jump all the way down her throat yet, Jane. I want her to be totally coherent when I really chew her out." Molly joined the other officers inside. Ari groaned and thought she might throw up.

"Did you see anything?" Jane whispered.

Ari shut her eyes. "No, he hit me before I could turn around."

"How do you know it was a *he*?"

She blinked and saw Deborah Thorndike coming after her with the poker. "I guess I just assumed." The throbbing in her head was getting worse. "You didn't see anyone leave, did you?"

"No. It was dark, and I had the radio going. I just wasn't paying much attention. After about fifteen minutes I started to get worried. It was really scary walking up to that house alone, and then finding you . . ." Jane's voice trembled, and she took Ari's face between her hands. "Listen to me. Leave this to the police. You're a real estate agent, dammit, not a private investigator. You're licensed to write contracts, not lurk around crime scenes."

"Lurk?"

Jane grinned, losing all seriousness. "Great word, huh? It was in my word-of-the-day calendar this morning."

It hurt to smile. "You're probably right, Jane."

"I know I am. But hey," she said, grasping her arm, "I think the detective's a dream, and she's definitely got it bad for you." Ari's body instantly warmed to the thought.

It wasn't long before Molly returned to the patio and stared at Ari, arms crossed, a serious expression on her face. "I'm taking you to the emergency room." Ari could tell there was no point in arguing.

Molly had to physically lift her into the Ford's high cab. The next two hours at the emergency room were a blur, and before she knew it, Molly was unlocking her front door and leading her to the couch. She watched the detective play nursemaid, fetching her prescription and making tea. When Ari was finally comfortable, Molly joined her on the couch and pulled out her notebook.

She remained silent throughout Ari's account of the attack, frowning several times in disapproval. "The important part was what I realized right before I got knocked out," Ari concluded, wrapping up the story. "Thorndike couldn't have written that message on the wall."

Molly shook her head. "Ari, we took the fingerprints. They're his, and his hand was covered in his own blood."

"Listen to me," she persisted. "It was the wrong hand. Michael Thorndike was left-handed."

Molly's face contorted as the information sunk in. "Are you sure?"

"I saw the pictures at his office, of him signing documents and pitching a baseball. His teammates called him Lefty. The killer stuck his hand in the blood and wrote the name, but he used the wrong one."

Ari could hear Molly audibly sigh. Her left leg began to

97

bounce, as she nervously contemplated. She still wasn't ready to believe. "I don't know. Thorndike could have used his right hand just because it was easier to maneuver, or he could have been ambidextrous."

"I don't buy it. If Michael Thorndike wrote *Robert* on the wall as he was dying, wouldn't the letters have sloped down rather than up because he was getting weaker, and he was in such a cramped space. Wouldn't that be more natural?" Before Molly could interject, Ari added, "And why did he write *Robert*, why not *Bob*? It's a lot shorter."

Molly listened carefully, visualizing it in her mind. "If all of this is true, then it really does mean someone wants your friend Bob Watson to take the fall." She shifted on the couch, tapping her pencil nervously on the notepad. "Then why move the body?" she asked.

Ari bit her nail. That was the big question. Another niggle was forming in her mind, but she couldn't focus while her head pounded. "I don't know," she said finally.

Molly exhaled. "Do you have anything to drink?" she asked, already heading for the kitchen.

"There's beer in the fridge," Ari said, "or if you prefer something stronger, there's some stuff above the sink."

When Molly returned, she was carrying a bottle of scotch and a coffee mug. "You can't have any in your condition, and yes, I know this isn't the proper glass." Ari acted as though she didn't care, but it was amazing how Molly could read her thoughts. Molly settled next to Ari and took a big gulp.

Ari grabbed her head as a shooting pain ripped through her skull, the effects of the attack colliding with the hangover that was developing.

"How are you feeling?" Molly asked, pulling Ari against her.

"I'm sure I'll be better in about ten minutes. Why don't you tell me about the investigation?"

Molly finished her scotch and with her free hand poured another. "You're probably the last person I should say anything to."

"When my dad was working on a case, he'd come home and bounce ideas off my mom. You know, get a different perspective. Maybe I could do that for you."

Molly toyed with the idea for a moment and sighed. It couldn't do too much harm, and Ari had found an important clue that she had missed, a fact that stung. "Here's what we know," she began. "Michael Thorndike was killed between eight and ten. Cause of death has been determined to be two shots from a thirty-eight." She stopped suddenly, mindful of the gun Andre had found, the one still being tested.

"What's your theory?"

"We think the killer lured Thorndike to the scene, but we don't know why. The back patio door was pried open, so most likely, the killer arrived first, let himself in and greeted Thorndike at the front door."

"Did you have my lockbox read?"

"Yes, and there was nothing unusual. All the codes checked out to other agents and service people."

"Are you sure that you can rule out all of them? Thorndike was very active in real estate. Maybe he made an enemy."

"It's possible, but it's really unlikely," Molly said with a dismissive gesture. "Why would a killer use his lockbox code and leave such an obvious clue?"

Ari knew she was right. "There's still something that's bothering me. Why did it happen in that house? In my listing?"

Molly stroked Ari's thick, black hair, rapidly losing interest in the conversation. "I don't think you're going to like it. The only thing I've been able to determine is that the killer has to be someone who knew the house was vacant. That would be your friends, Bob and Lily." Ari started to speak, but Molly held up her hand. "Don't get defensive. I'm just speaking logically. Premeditated murders don't happen just anywhere. The killer knows where to go."

"But according to Bob and Lily, several people knew about that house. Bob had mentioned it to his work associates, and Lily had been actively looking for buyers through her charity contacts. Even Deborah Thorndike could have known."

"How?"

"Both of them go to the same club, they probably play tennis together, go to aerobics. Anything is possible," she said. "Have you spoken with Deborah Thorndike?"

"Twice."

"And?" she pressed.

Molly's expression went blank. "And nothing. The woman's as cool as a cucumber. She says her husband was leaving her and she was learning to accept it. I'm totally suspicious of her just on those two points alone, but she has an alibi for the night of the murder. She was at the movies, and she had the ticket stub."

"That's pretty shaky," Ari commented.

Molly was nodding in agreement. "I know, but some concessions clerk remembered selling her popcorn. It's not a great alibi. She could have made sure someone saw her and then slipped out. But I'll tell you this, if that woman knows more about her husband's death, she's doing a great job stonewalling."

Ari didn't know how to tell Molly about her meeting with the widow. She withdrew from the detective's embrace and took a sip of tea. "First, Deborah Thorndike has not accepted her husband's abandonment, and second, that woman is capable of many things, not the least of which is murder."

"How do you know this?" Molly asked, staring hard at Ari.

"I talked with her."

Molly was shocked. "Where? When?"

"This afternoon at the Desert Racquet Club."

"What were you doing there?"

Half smiling she said, "I snuck in and met with her in the sauna. I got her to tell me the truth." She recounted their meeting, Molly's face clouding with concern as she reached the climactic moment with the hot poker in her face.

"Dammit, Ari!" Molly bellowed. "You have to stop doing this!"

Ari winced in pain, Molly's voice echoing throughout her brain. "I was in a public place," she argued feebly.

Molly ignored Ari's ploy for sympathy. "And that didn't stop her from nearly poking your eye out! What if those women hadn't come in? If you really think Deborah Thorndike is capable of killing her own husband, how hard do you really think it would be for her to drop someone she'd just met, someone who'd just lied to her?" Ari didn't have an answer. Molly emptied the scotch bottle into the mug and took a swig, watching Ari rub her head. Feeling a twinge of guilt, Molly started to massage Ari's neck and shoulders. "Tell me about Lily Watson," she said softly. "How much do you know about her?"

Ari laughed. "Lily? I don't think she killed Michael Thorndike."

"Why not? She was involved with him. Maybe she was mad because he dumped her."

"The truth is, Lily dumped Michael, and I don't think she ever stopped loving him," Ari stated.

"Then why did she dump him?"

"Because she was married to Bob," Ari said sharply.

"That didn't stop her from having an affair," Molly remarked.

Ari sighed. "You're right. I don't know what to think. Deborah Thorndike told me today that Michael was going to leave her for some woman he met through charity work. I'm beginning to think that Michael and Lily may have resumed their affair, especially if Bob was having an affair of his own."

The bombshell hit Molly and her jaw dropped open. "What?"

"I think Bob was having an affair with Kristen Duke. She all but told me so this morning when I talked to her."

Molly reached for her glass, the massage abandoned. "Let me see if I've got this straight. In the last twelve hours, you've spoken with Kristen Duke, been nearly seared by Deborah Thorndike and knocked unconscious. Is there anything else, Ari?"

Ari chewed on her nail. This was one of those difficult moments. She knew she should tell her potential love interest the truth, but she'd already pushed Molly to the edge of the trust precipice. Molly's eyes narrowed, and Ari hoped her candor wouldn't propel Molly from the condo. "Well, in between the Deborah Thorndike incident and going to the crime scene, Jane and I ran into Russ Swanson outside of Smiley's. That was just accidental, though," Ari quickly added. "We approached him and she mentioned I'd been concerned about Thorndike's murder, and he got really nervous, jumped in his car and took off."

"This was *before* you got knocked on the head?"

Suddenly Ari realized what Molly was driving at. "Yes, it was."

"And I know for a fact," Molly continued, "that Russ Swanson knew about the vacant house."

Ari's stomach churned at the possibility of what Molly was suggesting. Could Swanson have followed them from Smiley's to the house?

Molly watched Ari's face pale. Instead of blowing up again at Ari, she resisted the urge, and instead took her hand. "I take my job very seriously. I risk my life more than I'd care to admit, and you're doing it practically on a daily basis." Ari remained silent. "Let's talk about tonight. You're all alone in a deserted, dark house. Most likely you met the killer."

Ari started to shake and tears slid down her face. Molly pulled her close, her anger vanishing. They remained motionless for several minutes until Molly whispered, "Is there any family I should call? You were attacked tonight, Ari."

"No," came the simple reply.

"Do you speak with your father?" Molly asked gently.

"Not for a long time. Not since my mother's funeral."

"Do you have any brothers or sisters?"

"I'm the only one," Ari said in a voice that was barely audible. From years of interviewing suspects and witnesses, Molly knew that there was a story there, but she wasn't going to ask. She drew a deep breath and closed her eyes, Ari snuggled against her, their hearts beating in a pleasant rhythm. Molly wanted to know everything that she could about the woman she held in her arms, but she remained content, breathing in Ari's strawberry scented hair as she fell asleep.

When Ari awoke, her mouth was dry and the morning light enveloped the condo. She was lying on the couch, a blanket covering her. Molly was gone, but she'd left a note under the bottle of scotch. She blinked and attempted to focus on the flowing handwriting:

Aria, you are indeed beautiful music. As I write, I still feel the warmth of your embrace and the scent of your hair. I can't wait for tonight. Until then, try to stay out of trouble. I want a real first date.

—M.

Ari reread the words a dozen times, her face pressed against the blanket, breathing Molly's cologne. It took another half hour before she hoisted herself upright, a difficult task in itself. Her Grand Canyon-sized headache had turned into a dull throb. She could live with it and function.

The phone rang, a foghorn in her ear. She snatched it up before it could ring again.

"Hello," she grumbled.

"Ari, it's Bob."

Chapter Twelve
Wednesday, June 20
9:36 a.m.

"Bob, you've got to come back. You're only making it worse for yourself," Ari pleaded.

"No," he said. "I only called you because I knew you'd worry." His voice hurried through the sentence, and Ari guessed it would be a short conversation. As paranoid as Bob could be, he probably thought the call was being traced.

"Bob, have you talked to Lily? She's really concerned."

"She should be," he said, his tone filled with disgust.

Ari shook her head in surprise. "What do you mean?"

Realizing he had spoken sharply, he backtracked. "Nothing. Look, don't say anything to her. I'll call her soon."

"Tell me where you are. Let me help you."

"I can't, Ari. This is my problem, and I'll deal with it. You just need to stay out of it."

She absently touched the lump on the back of her head, a dull throbbing beginning at the back of her skull. "Bob, you need to turn yourself in."

"I can't right now," he said firmly.

"Why not? You're innocent, aren't you?" She was almost afraid of his answer.

He breathed deeply. "Ari, if you of all people have to ask that question . . ."

"No, I really don't," she said hastily. "I don't believe you killed anyone, and you need to come back and clear your name."

"Yeah, right. If they don't convict me for Thorndike's murder, they'll put me in jail for fleeing."

Since her appeal to friendship wasn't working, Ari switched tactics. Although Bob was an emotional person, he was also very logical. "What are you going to do? Run to South America? You can't hide forever."

"I have a plan, but I can't tell you what it is." He sighed audibly. "You're just going to have to trust me."

Ari felt sick. "A *plan*? A plan for what? Catching the killer? Are you crazy?"

"Ari, if I come back, they'll put me in jail," he repeated.

He was right. If he walked into the police station, Molly would arrest him, but Ari also knew a good attorney could probably get him out on bail, if he could prove Bob had left under duress and wouldn't do it again. It was risky. "Tell me where you are, Bob," she said evenly.

"No."

He was getting short with her, and he wanted to get off the phone. "Bob, are you having an affair with Kristen Duke?" The line was silent. She'd thrown him a curve ball. He didn't need to respond, because for Ari, a friend of twenty years, the silence was enough.

"Now's not the time to go into that. Just stay out of this, sweetie." Bob's voice was sincere. She heard the hard click and they were disconnected.

What Ari really wanted to do was crawl back into bed. The phone conversation had set off cannons in her head, she was emotionally spent from the attack and she just wanted to savor the memory of Molly snuggled against her. Unemployed, this was a day she could have easily made some tea and read the paper surrounded by the soft down pillows, Molly's musky scent lingering near her.

As much as her body wanted the rest, her mind was on overdrive, and a huge headache was inevitable, so she might as well try to get some answers from Lily. Questions filled her mind as the traffic snaked up Camelback Road. Bob had sounded angry with her for some reason, so did he suspect Lily was the killer or did he *know* she was the killer? Maybe he knew she was seeing Michael Thorndike again.

Her eyes jolted back to the road as the red taillights in front of her glared bright red. She automatically hit her brakes and the tires squealed. Glancing into her rearview mirror, the waving middle finger from the driver behind her was hard to miss. She accelerated again, but her thoughts easily drifted back to some of the images that had crowded her mind for the last few days: her father pulling her into a bear hug on the day she graduated from the police academy, her mother's emaciated body lying in a hospital bed while Ari held her hand, Molly Nelson's crystal blue eyes, Bob's concerned face looming over her and calling her name while she drifted in and out of a fog.

That was the image that kept her pursuing Michael Thorndike's killer, involving herself in something that could get her arrested and drive away a woman who absolutely fascinated her. She could lose so much, but she had no choice. *Have you ever owed a debt you never thought you could repay?*

Dance music blared from inside the Watson's ranch house, and she had to sit on the bell for almost a solid minute before

Lily abruptly opened the door. Her body was covered with a sheen of perspiration and her cheeks were crimson from the hard workout. She wore black spandex biking shorts and a lime green sports bra, her makeup perfectly applied. She stood there with her hands on her hips, revealing long maroon colored fingernails with specks of gold. Knowing Lily, she'd been pumping iron for over an hour, an activity Ari despised. Racquetball was enough. Fortunately, Ari's metabolism pitied her and she managed to stay in single-digit pant sizes. Still, she envied Lily's body and knew her arms and shoulders would never look as lean and toned as the short, sinewy woman in front of her.

"Oh, it's you," she said, relieved. "I thought it was that bitchy detective coming back for another round." She motioned for Ari to follow her into the house. Lily disappeared down the hallway and the music was silenced. She returned with a gym towel over her shoulders, sipping on a mineral water.

"Let's go sit out on the porch," Lily suggested. "Can I get you anything?"

"What you're drinking looks great."

They stopped in the kitchen long enough for Lily to retrieve another bottle and pull her auburn hair into a ponytail. She led Ari out to the backyard, which in Ari's opinion, was the best part of the house. The patio was paved completely in flagstone with a flower bed border, a huge built-in barbecue tucked in the corner. The crystal blue pool shimmered just a few feet away, surrounded by a lush green yard dotted with sculpted shrubbery.

Lily turned on the misters before joining Ari at the patio table. "I take it you haven't heard from Bob?" Ari asked expectantly.

"No," Lily said softly. The expression on her face was a cross between fear and anger. "He hasn't even called. I'm getting worried, Ari. We've always been so considerate of each other. Always calling, always home in time to kiss each other goodnight, or you know—" Lily blushed. "I'm worried something's happened to him. He should be home by now." Lily seemed afraid, but Ari had to wonder if it was fear of his whereabouts or fear that he might expose her. She pushed the thought away, not ready to accept that Lily was capable of murder.

"Lily, I remember how often Bob used to disappear. He's been leaving rooms since high school. It's his mode of defense."

"Not anymore," Lily disagreed.

"Do you think there's any possibility—"

"No!" she shouted. "Don't even say it! You know him, Ari. Bob could never kill anyone. It's not in his nature."

"Lily, I believe in Bob's innocence," she said calmly. "But there had to be a reason his name was written behind the bar. He did threaten Thorndike, right?"

Lily's face darkened and she shook her head furiously. "Those were only words. They didn't mean anything. Do you know what he did the next day? He called Michael and apologized." She leaned across the patio table for effect. "He apologized to the man who'd screwed his wife. Can you believe it?"

Ari switched topics, not knowing what else to say. "Tell me more about your relationship with Michael Thorndike."

Lily shifted uncomfortably in her chair. "There's really nothing more to tell. Michael pursued me. I hadn't been looking to have an affair, but it just happened. We were co-chairs of a fundraising luncheon at the Phoenician. Everyone had left and he invited me to take a stroll around the resort. I didn't realize he had a room." She stopped abruptly and blushed.

"How long did the affair go on?" Ari asked.

"You mean before Bob caught us? About six months. We'd meet at different places, but never at our homes. Sometimes hotels, sometimes offices that he owned. One time we even did it in a public bathroom."

This was more information than Ari needed to know. "So, after Bob discovered the two of you, then you just broke it off?"

Ari had trouble believing Lily could so easily dismiss a man she loved so much.

"Of course. Bob is my husband, and we're married." But that didn't stop you from bedding Michael Thorndike, Ari thought, remembering Molly's comment from the night before. "In the last two years I've only seen Michael a few times at different charity functions," Lily added.

"And you've never been alone with him?"

Lily's eyes turned cold. "What are you implying, Ari?"

"I'm not implying anything. I'm trying to establish that your relationship with Michael Thorndike is totally and completely over."

"It's over," Lily said, rising from the chair. "Now, if you'll excuse me, I need a shower. Between you and that Detective Nelson, I've been quizzed enough."

"Did she come by this morning?" Ari asked innocently.

"She comes by every morning, just to bait me. She asks me these questions, actually it's the same question over and over in a different way. Trying to see if I'll change my story."

"What does she want to know?" Ari asked, already knowing the answer.

Lily wiped some perspiration from her brow and closed her eyes. "She implies that I know where Bob is."

"And you don't?" Lily's nostrils flared, and Ari knew she'd asked one question too many.

"Show yourself out," Lily growled. She stomped back into the house while Ari finished her mineral water and thought about Lily's conflicted emotions. She said it was over, but when she spoke of Michael Thorndike, there was a dreamy quality in her eyes that betrayed her true feelings. If indeed she was still in love with Thorndike, then something happened and she killed him, or she must be devastated by his death.

The family room was empty when Ari went back inside. She

could hear the shower down the hall. Ari dropped her water bottle into the trash, noticing Lily's large bag on the counter, the edge of her planner protruding from the top. She knew Lily kept everything of value in that book. It was her life. She glanced once more down the hall, the sound of the water still going.

Carefully pulling the leather book from the bag so as not to dislodge the multitude of paper scraps that were jammed in between the pages, Ari flipped through the months, starting at the beginning of the year. By March, she noticed a pattern. Every Wednesday, the same time was penciled in—no name, just a time. She paged ahead to June and found the seventeenth. Lily had planned nothing on the day of Michael Thorndike's death. Ari rifled through the blank months yet to come, finding nothing except a cleaning at the dentist. She fingered the papers behind December, a sticky note stuck to the back cover. There in Lily's unmistakable handwriting, MICHAEL 6/10 @ 2:00 P.M. She reopened the planner and looked under June tenth. The square was blank.

She knew time was running short. A quick check through the bag revealed nothing unusual. Ari picked up the heavy planner to set it back as she'd found it, when she noticed a small, bulging zippered pocket attached to the wall of the purse. Inside were half a dozen condoms. Anyone who didn't know the Watsons might just assume they had an exciting love life, but Ari knew many important and intimate facts about both of them, one of which was Bob's sterility.

The shower abruptly stopped and silence filled the house. Ari dropped the planner into the bag and darted into the nearby laundry room. She pressed against the wall, her face peering around the corner as Lily entered the kitchen clad only in a towel. The significance of what she was doing suddenly hit her. She would have a very difficult time explaining this to Lily, and if in fact Lily was the killer, then Ari had a much larger problem.

The phone rang. Lily glanced at it and hesitated before

answering. Ari was sure everyone from close friends to nosy reporters had rung the phone off the hook. On the fourth ring she finally answered.

"Hello? Where the hell are you! The police are looking for you . . . Bob, please." Lily's voice rose in frustration. There was a long pause. "Bob, listen to me . . . Bob! . . . Shit! Hold on a sec . . ." Ari heard Lily fumbling around in the drawers, looking for a pen and then writing down information. "All right, I'm coming . . . I'm coming!" she shouted and hung up the phone.

Ari heard footsteps rush down the hallway and the bedroom door clicked shut. Ari retreated to her SUV and drove around the corner, knowing Lily would have to pass her. Feeling safe in her own vehicle, the panic she had experienced just five minutes before dissipated, replaced by another rush of adrenaline. She clicked the CD changer and the Indigo Girls filled the truck, while she enjoyed the surge of emotion. She hadn't felt this alive in a long time. While she loved real estate, the endless paperwork was mind-numbing, and the lack of respect pummeled her self-esteem on a weekly basis.

Her cell phone rang. She fumbled for it in her bag, her gaze focused on the tip of the Watsons' driveway.

"Yeah," she answered, sounding annoyed.

"Well, yeah to you, too," Jane said, matching her tone. "Where are you?"

"I'm out previewing houses."

Jane roared with laughter. "Sure you are. So what are you really doing?"

"I'm about to tail Lily. I think she's going to visit Bob." Ari couldn't hide the excitement in her voice.

"You're tailing Lily," Jane repeated. "Ari, maybe you've forgotten, but you gave up that career, and if you haven't noticed, your SUV isn't equipped with lights and a siren, and you don't get to wear those sleek black uniforms."

"Very funny, Jane." Suddenly Lily's Miata pulled out of the

111

drive. "I've got to go." Jane started to make another crack, but Ari flipped the cell phone closed.

Lily rounded the corner quickly and headed to the stop sign. When she turned on to Camelback Road, Ari shot to the sign and made a quick left, staying a safe distance behind Lily as the two vehicles wound around the base of Camelback Mountain. Named for its appearance, it really looked like a camel's back, but this camel carried the most expensive real estate in the city. The homes on the mountain housed sports figures, celebrities and countless other power brokers, all of whom enjoyed the desert views.

They continued west toward the freeway. The beautiful east side homes lining the busy thoroughfare gave way to the tall buildings of the Central Corridor and the business section of Phoenix. The landscape morphed the further they drove, and the housing prices plummeted. The west side had always struggled with poverty, and the decrepit storefronts, low budget mini-malls and street people increased in numbers as they approached the freeway entrance.

Although the morning rush hour was ending, Ari knew it would be easy to lose Lily in the heavy traffic, which never ceased at any time of day. Phoenix had indeed become a second Los Angeles, Ari thought, only hotter. For six miles, Ari strained to keep Lily in view as she maneuvered in and out of lanes, hurrying toward Bob. Just as the traffic was starting to thin, she abruptly put on her blinker and sped off the freeway. Ari signaled and moved right, noticing the east side of the freeway was lined with upscale accommodations, the kind Bob would choose. Cheap motels were not his style.

Lily continued down the freeway access road and turned into a place that looked more like a condo complex than a motel. Ari drove past the street and entered through the parking lot, threading her way through the cars. Once she rounded the corner, she stopped, not wanting to come upon the Miata suddenly. In the bottom of her stomach, she still had this nagging feeling she would be caught, that Lily would appear at any moment, tap on her window and end the pursuit.

Ari used a dumpster for camouflage and watched Lily stroll to the last building. She paused for a second, gauged her surroundings and disappeared. Ari edged the SUV to the end of the building just as Lily ascended the stairs to a second story unit. She knocked once, and the door opened swiftly and shut twice as fast.

Ari debated what to do. Lily could be in there for hours. Ari could leave and come back, now that she knew where Bob was staying, but that seemed risky. What if Lily was there to help him pack? Ari decided to wait it out. She drove around to the other side of the parking lot, placing her under Bob's window and in the opposite direction for Lily's eventual departure.

Within an hour, Ari's resolve was wavering, bored with the task and concerned by the ominous clouds starting to form. Soon the sky would turn a violent black-and-blue and the sky would open with lightning and downpours. She thought of her date with Molly and hoped the storm would push through before their scheduled hike.

Despite the cloud cover, it was still hot, the temperature inching up every minute. In Phoenix, monsoons only added to the misery by increasing the humidity. She'd turned the engine and air conditioning on and off three times, but it didn't help. She checked her watch and toyed with the idea of confronting them together, but she would feel outnumbered. She wanted Bob alone. Even during the course of their friendship, Lily had remained somewhat of an outsider, once describing herself that way to Bob. She would give Lily fifteen more minutes, and after that, she would retreat from the heat for an hour, heading over to a coffee shop she'd passed on the access road. Hopefully Bob wouldn't disappear again while she was slurping down a Diet Coke.

Just as she made the decision, the door opened and Lily

emerged. Judging from her animated gestures, Ari could tell she was upset, waving her arms, pointing to the parking lot. Bob stroked her shoulders and kissed her forehead. Ari assumed Lily was trying to talk him into going back, but it didn't work. She tore away from his embrace and walked away, her arms hugging her chest. Bob watched her go, and Ari watched Bob until he went back into the room and slowly shut the door.

Chapter Thirteen
Wednesday, June 20
11:18 a.m.

The first monsoon of the season swept through the Valley of the Sun, causing multiple accidents, flooding low-lying areas and knocking out power lines. Molly knew someone would likely die during one of nature's most unpredictable storms. Monsoons appeared with little warning, even on clear days. Hikers started up Camelback Mountain and were stranded by the time they reached the top. U.S. 60 crawled to a halt as Phoenicians, paranoid about any rain whatsoever, became overly cautious in the downpour.

Molly marveled at the charcoal colored haze, lightning stabbing the skyline every few seconds and thunder roaring in the distance. From inside the Emporium, the show was even more incredible, viewed through the expansive skylight and glass walls, the sounds of the storm echoing through the empty building. Molly had never seen the Emporium before, and the only word she could find to describe it was *spectacle*.

Even without the usual interior design touches like greenery or sculptures, wealth oozed from the baseboards to the cathedral ceilings. Tenants and clients would be immediately impressed by the immense black marble reception counter that stood as a sentry facing the front doors. If one were lucky enough to pass muster, she could advance to the bank of four shiny elevators waiting to take passengers upward to places of success and power. Should she have to cool her expensive loafers on the Italian tile, she could relieve any accumulated stress of the day by watching the indoor fountain, complete with waterfalls and koi pond.

A loud ding filled the lobby as the elevator closest to Molly opened. She hesitantly stepped on, aware that the building was like a Beverly Hills version of a ghost town, and she was completely alone.

She pressed four and ascended quickly and smoothly to the top floor, instantly understanding why only the truly lucrative and cash rich businesses could have afforded the Emporium's exorbitant rents. The investors had assumed every powerful Scottsdale firm would flock to the plush carpets, thick oak doors and prime location.

But no one came. A few egotistical status seekers weathered the first year, but when no one joined them to fill the dozens of offices, they too abandoned the Emporium and sought more affordable quarters. Maybe that was why the rich kept getting richer, Molly thought, as she wandered down corridors large enough to park a semi. They didn't want the best—they wanted a deal.

By the time she returned to the lobby, her jaw hurt from gaping at the size of the place, and she was convinced Michael Thorndike was right. She was certainly not a contractor, but with

116

some renovation and changes, the Emporium would have made a great museum.

"Pretty spectacular, huh?" the voice called out from the second floor balcony. She looked up and saw Felix Trainor leaning against the railing. He bounded down the spiral staircase, his silk tie flapping back and forth. He looked more like a young college student than a savvy millionaire. Molly glanced at her watch, actually glad that he was fifteen minutes late and not present for her little self-guided tour.

Standing next to her he looked even younger, and he was definitely shorter by nearly half a foot. They both turned their heads upward as thunder crashed around them, the monsoon engulfing the building. "It's extraordinary," Molly admitted.

"Too expensive," Trainor commented. "To a businessman, it's all about profit-and-loss margin. They don't care much about how anything looks except the bottom line."

Molly felt a lecture coming on. "Mr. Trainor, you're the one who asked me to meet you out here, and I hope it wasn't just to look at architecture."

He nodded and pressed his lips together. "I wanted to talk to you alone, away from the other partners. What you saw and heard at that meeting was controlled civility. None of those people cared much for Michael, especially Florence Denman."

Molly sifted through her list of alibis, and Denman had a solid one: the guest speaker at a business dinner. Two hundred sets of eyeballs could verify her whereabouts during the time Michael Thorndike was shot. Still, she could have hired someone. "Was she jealous?"

Felix snorted. "Absolutely. Michael was the head of the League, the founding member. He got all the press, and he was the most creative and innovative, the golden boy."

"So they all envied him," Molly summarized.

"Yes," Trainor agreed, "but Florence had a more personal

reason for disliking Michael Thorndike. You see, they had an affair, and he dumped her for someone else."

"Someone else besides his wife," Molly clarified.

"I think his wife was probably the one woman he *wasn't* sleeping with in this town," he cracked.

Molly was surprised at Trainor's change of attitude. "Okay, so Florence Denman had a personal reason to dislike Michael Thorndike, but you're suggesting the other partners disliked him, too?"

"Absolutely. They hated the fact that he was the most powerful."

"Except you."

The statement didn't faze him as it would most. He stuck his hands in his expensive pants pockets and looked her in the eye. "I respected Michael immensely. Some people even spread trash that I was in love with him—which I wasn't," Trainor quickly added.

"But the fact is, Michael had an incredible knack for making money. Every project he undertook made me very wealthy. I don't have a problem with that, and I don't have a problem giving him the credit for it," he said with a self-deprecating gesture. "I'm thirty-eight years old and a multimillionaire." His face flushed against his deep tan and humility returned. "My point is, for the other partners, wealth wasn't enough. They couldn't be grateful. They were jealous of his power and abilities."

"But is jealousy enough of a reason to kill?" Molly interjected. She didn't need a speech on the great Michael Thorndike.

Trainor smiled condescendingly, as if Molly was a child about to learn a lesson. "Detective Nelson, do you think fifty million dollars is a lot of money?"

Molly checked the dark sky above and her growing impatience. She had a pile of reports to read and several other things to do, and the drive back to Phoenix would consume another precious thirty minutes of her evaporating day. "Mr. Trainor, I'm really not in the mood for games," she said curtly.

He looked downward. "Sorry, stupid question." He shifted his feet and changed his expression. "Michael wanted to save the Emporium. The price tag was fifty million dollars. Spending that much would have greatly compromised the League's cash flow."

"You mean bankrupt it?" Molly clarified.

Trainor's eyes narrowed, doing the mental calculations. Molly could tell he wasn't prone to exaggeration. "Parting with that much money would have made us very vulnerable." Molly nodded. "Cy and Flo didn't want to spend it, but it didn't matter. Michael is"—he corrected himself—"*was* the head of the League. He had a vote and Sorrel and I agreed with him."

Even without a college degree, Molly could do the math. A tie. She sensed she knew what was coming. "Who breaks the tie, Mr. Trainor?"

Felix smiled at her business acumen. "Exactly as you would expect, Detective Nelson. Whichever side Michael voted for won in the event of a tie." Molly sighed, realizing that the suspects on her list were multiplying like hamsters. "So in answer to your initial question, would jealousy be enough to kill? Probably not. But fifty million dollars would."

Chapter Fourteen
Wednesday, June 20
1:14 p.m.

At the sight of Ari, Bob's face changed from shock to resignation quickly. He stepped away from the door and Ari walked to the middle of the spacious living area, gaining a view of the entire place. Clothes were strewn everywhere, pizza boxes littered the tables and bags of groceries lined the kitchen counters. Lying in the center of the bed was the day's newspaper, open to an article about the Thorndike case. Molly was right. Someone was helping Bob, most likely his mistress, Kristen. Their eyes met and he looked away, embarrassed. His body dropped into the couch. He looked thinner, and his rumpled T-shirt and shorts hung loosely over his large frame.

"How did you find me?" The question left his mouth like a deflating tire.

"I did some checking," Ari lied. Relaying the circumstances that led her there would not be advantageous.

He made a disgusted sound and the silence resumed. "Are you afraid of me, Ari? Do you think I did it?" She shook her head no, unable to form a response. "Now you know why I'm hiding." Bob threw his hands up in the air for emphasis. "If one of my oldest friends, and my wife," he added, motioning to the door, "think I'm a murderer, what will the cops believe?"

"How long were you planning on hiding?" Ari asked, seeing an opening for conversation.

"I don't know. I was trying to figure things out."

"You've made it worse by running. There's been a manhunt for you since Sunday."

Bob's face reddened. "How much worse could it get?" He went to the bed and picked up the paper, assessing the details and damage from the news. "My name is scrawled on a wall, for God's sake! How much worse can it get!" He crushed the paper and threw it across the room. The sudden violent outburst brought a sliver of doubt back into Ari's brain.

"Bob, tell me again about that night. You were with Kristen, right?"

He shot her a warning look at the mention of his lover's name before answering, "Yes, and she left around eight thirty." Bob paced back and forth in front of the couch, his hands shoved in his pockets, much like a caged animal, Ari thought.

"Did any customers come into the store after Kristen left?"

"No, we close at eight. I was going over some paperwork."

"Did anyone see you leave at ten?"

"I doubt it. On Saturday nights Mill Avenue is packed. I'm not that memorable."

Ari pressed her hands to her temples, trying to will away her growing headache. She still sensed Bob wasn't being truthful, but she didn't want to push him too hard. Grasping at straws, she asked, "Did you stop anywhere? Like a convenience store, or a gas station?"

121

"I was alone!" Bob yelled, causing Ari to jump. He instantly softened. "I'm sorry, Ari. I shouldn't be yelling at you. You're only trying to help."

There was a lot Ari didn't like about the conversation, but Bob's temper coupled with his inability to meet her gaze made her nervous and scared. She stepped in front of Bob and looked him squarely in the eye. "Bob, I've known you most of my life, and I've never lied to you. Now I'm asking you the same. Tell me you had nothing to do with Michael Thorndike's death."

His lips quivered as he barely held his composure. "I swear it. I could never lie to you." Her face must have still held some doubt, because he took her face between his hands and added, "We've been through too much." Knowing exactly what he meant, all of Ari's doubt vanished forever, and she hugged him tightly.

"You need to turn yourself in," she said softly. "If I can find you, I'm sure the police can follow the trail of bread crumbs. I won't lie to you, Bob, the police will find you, because this isn't a movie. And when they do, you've seriously jeopardized your chances for bail. I can guarantee you that if the cops bring you in, you'll spend your time in the Madison Street Jail with some real winners." Ari thought that would convince him. A man who couldn't see himself in a cheap motel certainly couldn't fathom a county cell.

Surprisingly, Bob shook his head adamantly and started pacing. "No, there's no way." He stared at her seriously. "There's more to this than you know, including things I can't tell you."

"What things?" Ari asked, totally frustrated and baffled. Bob was not a stupid person, but he was on the verge of ruining his entire life by hiding from the police. She knew he understood this. "Are you protecting Kristen?"

At the mention of her name, his eyebrows furrowed and his face hardened. "Leave her out of this, Ari."

His tone challenged her, and she was in no mood for it. She

was here to help, and Bob was being too stubborn for his own good. "She's the one who is helping you, right?"

Bob scowled. "Don't give me that disapproving tone! You're the last one to judge my girlfriend," he retorted, his finger pointed at her.

Ari threw up her hands, ready to scream. The worst thing about fighting with best friends was that they knew your past, and Ari knew Bob was referring to Breanna, Ari's third serious girlfriend who was barely eighteen when Ari seduced her. It was one of Ari's greatest regrets, and it only angered her more that Bob was throwing it in her face. She went to the phone and picked up the receiver. Very calmly she said, "If you do not give me some honest answers right now, I'm turning you in."

Bob looked at the phone, knowing she was serious. "Okay, here's the whole truth. All of it." He raised his right hand, as if swearing on a Bible. "Yes, Kristen and I are having an affair, and I'm in love with her." He gauged Ari's reaction, but she remained neutral.

"It started about four months ago. She's a wonderful person, mature beyond her years. She's actually more mature than Lily," he added. "We spent a lot of time talking. We like the same authors, the same art. I started to find reasons to be at the Tempe store." He looked up, wanting reassurance. Ari nodded and he continued. "She came on to me, because I don't think I ever would have done anything about it. Then things progressed from there," he said with a little laugh. "I didn't mean for it to happen, but Kristen is very persuasive, and to be honest, I was flattered. A young, hot girl interested in me? It was really amazing."

"Does Lily know?"

Bob shook his head. "No. She doesn't have a clue."

"Are you sure, Bob? Lily is very intelligent and observant. I'm having a lot of trouble believing she doesn't know."

He was still shaking his head. "Ari, the woman is talking about renewing our vows next year for our fifteenth wedding anniversary. There's no way she knows and frankly, I don't think she believes I'm the type to cheat."

"Neither did I," Ari said, instantly regretting the comment when Bob's face darkened.

"I'm going to take care of this in my own way, and now you need to go and pretend you were never here," he said in a hushed tone, and Ari knew there was nothing she could say that would change his mind.

She chewed her nail, debating what to do, the wheels of her mind constructing all the scenarios. She would always be a cop, and the daughter of a cop, someone who upheld the law. "And I suppose you're going to ask me just to keep quiet and not say anything," Ari commented, clearly perturbed. She looked away, unable to look him in the eye, angry as hell but waiting for the request.

Bob crooked his finger under her chin and turned her face until their eyes met. "I'm not *asking*, Ari. You owe me." She stared at him, unable to speak. *Have you ever owed a debt you could never repay?*

Ari closed her eyes and sighed. It took twelve years, but Bob had finally called in his marker, the one hold he had over her and her sense of justice. What would she say to Molly? How could she face her?

"Fine," she said, with a touch of anger, agreeing to be silent, agreeing to break her promise to Molly. She knew her love life was ruined, and her debt, the only real debt she had in her life, was paid in full.

Chapter Fifteen
Wednesday, June 20
7:22 p.m.

Perched on a rock at the top of Squaw Peak, the purples, blues and yellows of a desert sunset made living in Phoenix totally worthwhile, Molly thought. Of course, she would have to ignore the thick layer of smog that hung at the bottom of the picture and made her wish she possessed the world's largest vacuum. Despite the brown cloud, the view from the valley's tallest mountain was breathtaking. All of Phoenix rested below them in four different directions, the western sky exploding in color. She leaned back on the rock they were sharing and placed her hand against the small of Ari's back. They were not alone, twenty other hikers making the grueling one-mile trek up the switchbacks as payment for the sunset. The afternoon monsoon proved to be a quick drenching that departed as fast as it had appeared. By seven thirty the trail had dried from the strong summer sun.

"It definitely makes me believe in God, or something," Ari murmured, admiring the final moments of daylight.

Molly stared at her face, tanned and flushed with color from the hike. "Absolutely beautiful," she replied.

Still looking out at the horizon, a smile crept on Ari's lips. "Detective, are you watching the sunset?" Molly answered by surreptitiously stroking Ari's thigh. She knew something was bothering Ari the moment she showed up at her door, but Ari told her it was just a little concern over being newly unemployed, a plausible explanation, but one Molly doubted. She let it go since it was their first date.

They made it back to the car in half the time it took to climb up, the beauty of gravity at work. "Now where?" Ari asked playfully.

"Tassoni's?" Molly suggested.

Ari nodded her agreement at the mention of her favorite pizza place. Complete with outdated furniture and a politically incorrect policy that allowed smokers to light up where they pleased, Tassoni's relied strictly on its strength: good food. Since it was a weekday, it wasn't crowded, and one of the dark, leather booths was available. Smoke wafted through the air, mixing with the unmistakable odor of oregano. The older waitress scribbled their order, not batting an eye at the two women holding hands across the table. Tassoni's shared a strip of property with After Hours, a lesbian bar, and the two places ensured each other's livelihood.

They chatted about the typical topics that naturally filled a first date, setting ground rules that the name Michael Thorndike was off limits. Molly couldn't believe she did most of the talking. Usually her dates had to pry information out of her like a bad interview on the *Today* show, but Ari asked all the right questions, and Molly found herself freely talking about her family. Her very protective brothers had no problem with her lesbianism and insisted on meeting her potential girlfriends, none of whom had ever remained in her life without their approval.

"So what would they think of me?" Ari asked.

Molly nibbled on her pizza crust and studied the beautiful woman across from her, an amused expression on her face. She could just picture all four of her brothers lapping the floor with their tongues over Ari.

"Why don't we find out? Why don't you come with me to dinner on Friday?" Ari blinked, clearly surprised. "Of course," Molly backpedaled, "if you're not ready for that, well then we could just wait a while. I mean it is only our first date, and you might find my family a little overwhelming."

"Why?"

Molly cut two more slices of the pie and chose her words carefully. "It's just that we're loud and rowdy, and when we're all together, it kind of looks like an obnoxious version of the Waltons." She glanced at Ari who still looked puzzled. "I'm just concerned because you don't have any siblings."

Ari twirled her wine glass by the stem, intently studying the motion. After several revolutions, she said, "I had a brother." More twirling. Back and forth. "He was shot during a convenience store holdup. He'd walked down to the corner convenience store to buy baseball cards. He didn't even know what was going on until he got close to the counter and saw the gun. He yelled or called out or something, I don't know. Later, the guy said Richie had surprised him. He thought he was alone in the store, but anyway, he turned and fired without even looking. When the police got there, it was too late. He was still holding his allowance and the baseball cards in his hand."

Molly sighed deeply. "Is that why you became a cop?"

Ari nodded, her mind drifting to the crime photos she'd found on her father's desk so many years ago. She'd snuck into his den and found the black-and-white blowups of her brother's body. "Actually, that was only part of the reason. I guess I wanted to please my father. After Richie died, he channeled all of his energy toward me. And later, I knew I wanted to help prevent other people from suffering the way my family had." A cynical expression covered her face. "At least that's what my shrink told me."

"So why did you quit?"

The answer to that question would take longer than eating a slice of pizza. The restaurant would have been dark for hours and any romantic fire would have been extinguished before she finished her story. "Too much pain and suffering," she said simply.

Molly squeezed her hand and replied, "I know." During the last ten years there were days Molly actually felt her heart harden at the sight of a murder victim or a molested child. It was a defense mechanism she switched on and off regularly, numbing her emotions in the process. She'd done the mental math long ago, adding the benefits of the job and subtracting the detrimental psychological effects. The sum total was a rationalization she'd learned to live with. Obviously, Ari had not.

Molly watched Ari drain her wineglass, her mind still lost on her family. Molly realized that she and Ari were both alone, but she was lucky to have her family. They couldn't keep her warm at night, but their support kept her going.

"Hey," Molly whispered.

Ari looked up from her glass, her face turning as red as the wine she'd finished. "I'm sorry. We should probably change the subject. What would you like to talk about?"

Molly cleared her throat. "Actually, there's something I want to do with you." Her eyes twinkled, and she smiled seductively.

"Oh?"

Molly threw some bills on the table and led Ari outside, turning toward the gay bar.

"Do you like to dance?" Molly asked, as a Bob Seger tune drifted into the parking lot.

Ari laughed and allowed Molly to lead her into the club and to the dance floor. Several women turned and glanced at them, the sole dancers.

"We're not exactly dressed to kill," Molly noted, their tall, sweaty bodies clad in shorts, tank tops and hiking boots.

Ari didn't care. She and Molly gyrated and twirled, and Ari realized she hadn't felt this free or uninhibited in a long time. The songs changed again and again, but Ari didn't want to stop. She and Molly moved to the beat together, their bodies inches apart. Ari was totally aroused by *not* touching Molly. Two more songs played, and Ari realized she couldn't stand it any longer. As a Madonna tune faded out, Ari grabbed Molly's belt and planted a kiss on her mouth.

The effect was immediate. Molly took Ari in her arms, her lips and tongue on fire.

"Hey, let's play one for the lovers on the dance floor," the DJ announced. A slow kd lang tune wailed over the speakers and bounced around the tiny square footage.

Molly released Ari, and they slowly circled, Molly unsure of what do with her two left feet. She smiled at Ari, feeling like a big dumb oaf. Fast dancing was one thing, but this required actual skill. Ari smiled back and pulled Molly against her, both conscious of their breasts and thighs colliding to the beat, gestures too sexual to be misunderstood. Ari's hands wandered down Molly's back, her fingers resting inside the waistband of Molly's shorts.

Molly groaned and squeezed Ari's buttocks, leaving no doubt about her growing wetness or her intentions. "We'd better get out of here," she said, "before I have to arrest myself for lewd and lascivious conduct."

Ari slammed the apartment door shut and shoved Molly against it. The detective had worked her hormones into a frenzy during the drive to Molly's place, stroking her thigh and working closer to her crotch with every passing mile. She was in no mood for tenderness, and thankfully, Molly wasn't either, both of them frantically working buttons and kicking off hiking boots.

"Yes," Molly murmured, before Ari buried her tongue in the woman's mouth and pressed against her, their bodies melding together perfectly, their hips finding an erotic rhythm. Ari drank in Molly's scent—lust, sweat and a fleeting hint of the musky cologne Ari loved. They were back on the mountain, climbing higher and higher, Ari's heart pounding in her chest, unable to breathe and feeling lightheaded from the rush. Her head lolled back and she whimpered. Higher and higher, closer and closer.

Molly's eyes were riveted to Ari's expression. Watching her face shift from pleasure to total abandon brought Molly to the edge of climax. "Come with me," she whispered, cupping Ari's buttocks, positioning Ari's center squarely against her own. "Now," Ari commanded, unable to prevent the rushing wave overtaking her body.

Molly thrust her pelvis against Ari one last time before she lost control and the orgasm rocked her body. Ari cried out at the same moment and every muscle tensed in response. Her fingernails dug deep into Molly's back as she held on, her head filling with bright colors.

Somehow Molly carried her to the couch and they stretched out, lying in each other's arms. Ari's whole body tingled and they remained still, listening to each other's heartbeats. When the room stopped spinning and she could breathe again, Ari surveyed the apartment, her eyes instantly drawn to the black baby grand piano that sat in the middle of the room. Everything else was inconsequential. The few pieces of furniture Molly owned were either family rejects or garage sale purchases. Two cheap nature prints hung on the walls, one too high and the other too low. A bookcase made of planks and bricks sat in the corner, a framed family photo on top next to a CD player. It was an interior designer's nightmare and paled in comparison to Ari's *House Beautiful* masterpiece.

Without uttering a word, Ari broke from Molly's embrace.

Molly watched her circle the piano and settle on the bench, running her fingers lightly across the keys from one end to the other. The sight of Ari, naked, glowing from sex, and leaning across her prized possession, refueled her desire.

Unaware of her effect on the detective, Ari innocently asked, "How long have you been playing?"

"Since I was a kid."

Ari's amazement grew. "You must be really good."

Molly shrugged off the compliment. "I don't know. I was never in any competitions or recitals, so I've never had anyone to compare myself to. I just play because I like to play."

"Would you play for me?" Ari asked.

Molly stared at Ari, her head cocked to one side, her black hair cascading over the finished wood, almost as if she were a part of the instrument. She joined her on the bench, and poised her hands over the keys, closing her eyes.

Ari watched Molly's fingers sail across the keys, mesmerized by the music that suddenly floated around the room. Pictures of her family, friends and past lovers flashed in her mind, a slide show for which Molly provided the music.

The music grew in intensity and tears streamed down Ari's cheeks, for her father, her brother, her mother, each of the women who had left her—all gone, but mostly for Molly, who would most certainly leave her once she learned of her deception. Ari let her mind focus on the crescendos and their evening, what would most likely be their only evening together. The music ended abruptly before Ari could contain her emotions.

"I didn't realize I was that bad," Molly said, wiping away Ari's tears with her palm.

"No," was all Ari whispered. Then she added, "I don't know much about instrumental music. Who's the composer?"

"I am," she said with a slight grin.

"You wrote that?" Ari asked. "It's incredible. Does it have a title?"

Molly blushed. "I call it *Aria*." Ari's eyes widened in surprise.

Molly cupped the beautiful woman's face in her hands and kissed her. She pulled away long enough to say, "I can't stop thinking about you. Every time I've sat down to play this week, I've only seen your face."

The sentiment melted Ari's heart and her promise to Bob seemed irrelevant, based on a debt from the past that at the moment she couldn't remember. The words formed in her mouth and just as she was about to betray Bob, Molly smothered her with a kiss that forced the confession back into Ari's throat and her body down on to the piano bench. Molly hovered over her, gently parting her legs and massaging her inner thigh.

Forgetting her battling conscience for the moment, Ari asked, "How many other women have you written music for?"

"Only you," Molly said, her index finger trailing down Ari's abdomen to the edge of her black patch. Ari's eyes remained glued to Molly's progress, her breath ragged from excitement. Molly's finger disappeared and Ari's mind emptied all its thoughts, lost in the detective's touch.

"Deeper," Ari murmured. Molly complied and Ari gasped. A cry forced itself out of her mouth. She had no idea when the moans subsided, only that Molly held her, still gently exploring, touching her with a tenderness she had never experienced.

Chapter Sixteen
Thursday, June 21
6:18 a.m.

The sunlight crept across the room as morning arrived. Molly smiled as her thigh passed over a damp patch of sheet. Ari stirred and pulled her closer, a sound of contentment emitting from her lips. "You didn't sleep much," Ari mumbled.

"*We* didn't sleep much," Molly corrected, an observation that made Ari chuckle. Molly stared at Ari's body, remembering every caress.

As incredible as the sex had been, for Molly the best part was wrapping her arms around Ari, their legs entwined, creating a human blanket. They had slept that way all night, Molly dead tired from waking up every hour. She couldn't fall into a deep sleep, afraid if she did, that Ari would slip from the sheets and out the door. She kept a still watch, her head buried in the soft silk of Ari's hair, touching her creamy skin, amazed that the beautiful woman was actually in her bed.

"I'll be right back," Molly said, staggering toward the bathroom.

Ari's eyes followed the naked detective's backside until the bathroom door swung shut. She blinked, waking up in more than one way. Last night was an escape, truly one of the greatest nights in her life, but with the morning came reality, the end of a dream vacation. She had not told Molly about Bob and the hand of deception rested on her shoulder, weighing her down, reminding her of what she had promised, and now, what she had done. She wanted to throw her clothes on and run out, but the door opened and Molly emerged, more beautiful than ever, and Ari suddenly wanted to be held, conscious that she'd been alone in the bed for a few minutes.

Molly dropped in front of Ari and took her hand. "My fragile ego has to know if you enjoyed last night."

"Enjoyed it?" Ari said with a laugh. "If I'd known how great sex was with a pianist, I would have gone after Kathy McMillan in high school."

Her tension eased, Molly joined in the laughter. "Who was she?"

"She played the organ for the school choir."

Molly shook her head and climbed back into bed. "Not as good. Organists don't have the same spread," she observed, holding out her right hand.

"God that's so sexual," Ari said, her eyes focused on Molly's long fingers. Molly snuggled against her, kissing her shoulders, whispering in her ear, informing her of several other things she wanted them to try, things she had thought about during her restless night. Ari showed her interest by rolling on top of Molly and letting her tongue roam across most of the detective's body. Only an hour later, when Molly's pager went off, did they reluctantly get out of bed. Molly had to get downtown immediately.

Sometimes it was just dumb luck that broke a case. A cop would pull a driver over for a broken taillight and find a dead body in a trunk. All the legwork and analysis couldn't replace a twist of fate. When it happened, Molly always thought of it as early karma for the criminal and a break for her. She didn't have any pride. If providence could solve a crime, who was she to argue?

She'd actually hoped they'd get lucky with the Michael Thorndike case, but doubted it would happen, simply because it rarely did. So when Andre paged her with a 911 saying there had been an anonymous tip about Bob Watson's whereabouts, she was skeptical. She felt a little guilty about not telling Ari the truth about where she was going. But the fact was, Ari was a civilian and had no business in the midst of her investigation. At least that's what she told herself as she raced north on the freeway, her mind sifting through the facts Andre had mentioned on the phone. He'd been so excited, and she laughed when she thought of him spewing information so fast that she couldn't write it all down. He'd sounded like a kid at Christmas.

He'd headed out early that morning to ask Russ Swanson questions about Speedy Copy's bank statements and some questionable withdrawals after learning that Bob Watson didn't handle any aspect of the finances. As he pulled out of a coffee shop, the anonymous call came into the precinct. They patched the caller through, who Andre could not identify as a man or a woman, but who said he or she knew that Bob Watson was staying at an upscale motel on I-17.

Molly inadvertently floored the gas, the needle shooting up to eighty. While she liked Andre, the fact that he got the call, and maybe Watson himself, bothered her. She was only five minutes behind him, cruising in the car pool lane, avoiding the rush hour traffic. Her thoughts bounced between her night with Ari and arresting Bob Watson. She had to laugh at the way her mind worked, one minute remembering the procedural manual and the next envisioning her legs spread open, Ari's silky tendrils of hair covering her abdomen while the real estate agent pleasured her.

Up ahead, Molly could make out the roadside sign for the motel. She deftly zipped across four lanes of traffic and focused on her driving. It didn't take much detective work to locate the two patrol cars and Andre's unmarked Cavalier, all three vehicles huddled in a corner of the property, one of the room doors wide open. She sensed something was wrong immediately. A look inside the comfortable suite confirmed her suspicions and sent her stomach into freefall. Bob Watson was gone, and Captain Ruskin would feast on her for lunch. The patrolmen and Andre avoided her gaze, knowing she would endure the wrath for losing Watson again. They gave Molly a wide berth as she toured Bob Watson's hiding place for the last four days, opening cabinets and checking drawers, finding any clues to his new location or his possible crime. Molly doubted they would find anything.

Her anger reached an apex as she stared into an empty closet. Andre drew near to her, holding a plastic baggy. "We found this on the counter," he said. Molly looked at the piece of motel stationary and the simple message written in black ink: *I am innocent.*

She glanced back into the closet. "He knew we were coming," she growled, stalking back into the kitchen. "All that's left is his worthless trash," she said motioning through the heap the officers had lain out on the kitchen table.

"Not quite," one of the officers said, holding up a rectangular piece of paper with some tweezers.

Molly recognized the logo from a distance before she read it, because she had a similar one in her wallet—Ari's business card, only hers didn't have the business phone scratched out. The importance of that simple blue line hit Molly in the gut. She stared hard at the card before turning to Andre. "I want you to find Russ Swanson—*now*," she said, pocketing the business card and heading for the door.

"Where will you be?" he called to her, but she was out the door.

Possibly arresting my lover, she thought.

Chapter Seventeen
Thursday, June 21
11:10 a.m.

It had not been a good morning for Ari. When the appraiser called on one of her properties, she knew it wasn't good. Her sellers had demanded a higher price than what it was worth. She had warned them it might not appraise, but as she hung up the phone and faced the prospect of telling them the bad news—she knew they would blame her, the perpetual scapegoat.

She called them immediately. There was a lot of swearing, mainly in Spanish, and although she could wander through a conversation, she wasn't fluent and only caught part of the dressing down they gave her. Eventually the punctuated language ceased, and they listened to the options, but it consumed an hour of her time and sent her hunting for aspirin and relaxation on her balcony.

She almost didn't hear the phone ringing over the traffic from the street below. "Hello?" she mumbled.

"Ari Adams?"

"Yes?" she answered, her finger over the flash button, ready to cut off the voice after her next sentence. She hated phone solicitors, although she was one herself.

"My name is Lorraine Gonzales, and I'm the acting broker for Southwest Realty."

"Oh, hello." Ari relaxed. It was just someone who wanted to know about one of her listings. She was reaching for her briefcase as she asked the standard question, "Which listing did you want to know about?"

The woman laughed. "Well, actually, all of them."

"I don't understand."

"I heard you quit Allstar and made that bastard Harry Lewis look absolutely ridiculous." Lorraine started laughing and Ari imagined she'd heard the details of the explosion. "Listen, chica, I want you to come for an interview," she stated directly, her rich, Spanish accent getting thicker with each sentence. "I've got a small company, but we do some big deals. I'm not into any games. I'm straight with my people and everybody gets along great. We're like a family and that's not bullshit. So, how about an interview?"

Ari smiled at the prospect of working for a woman and someone who shared her opinion of Harry Lewis. "I'd love to," she answered and she meant it.

"Terrific! And maybe you'll tell me what it was like finding Michael Thorndike's body."

"How did you hear about that?"

"I keep my ear to the ground, chica. That's why I'm the best, and that's why you should work for me." She took a breath and changed the subject. "That Michael Thorndike was quite a mover. I do some commercial, but nothing on his level. You know, he was trying to purchase the Emporium."

Ari was stunned. "No, I didn't know that. The League was going to buy it?"

"That's what I hear. Michael wanted to turn it into a museum. Apparently, he was strong-arming his partners into seeing things his way," she added. "Can you come in Monday at nine in the morning?"

"That's fine," Ari agreed absently.

"Our address is in the book, so I'll see you then," Lorraine said, cutting the connection. Ari stared at the receiver, pleasantly surprised by the opportunity that had just materialized, but more interested in Lorraine Gonzales's bombshell about the Emporium. The financial implications were enormous, so much so that someone might kill over it.

She was still pondering the situation twenty minutes later when the doorbell rang. Ari absently opened it without bothering to look through the peephole. The shiny badge caught her eye first, its wearer a somber-faced Tim Greer, an old family friend. Her brain connected this information in the time it took Molly to storm past her and into the center of the living room.

"Where is he?" she demanded, hands on her hips.

"Who?" was all Ari said, still confused about Tim's presence and Molly's abrupt mood shift from a few hours before.

A flicker of discomfort crossed Molly's face. "Tim, look around out here. I need to talk to Ms. Adams alone." Without an invitation, Molly stalked into Ari's bedroom, checked the closet and adjoining bathroom. A bewildered Ari followed her, mouth agape.

"What are you doing?" she finally thought to ask. Molly took the business card from her pocket and dropped it on the bed. It was hers, that much registered, but it didn't explain Molly's behavior. "I still don't understand, honey. Why are you so upset?"

"We found it this morning in a trash can at the Residence Inn out on the interstate." At the mention of the motel, Ari's face paled, a fact not lost on Molly. "An anonymous caller tipped us off that Bob Watson was staying there. Unfortunately, when we arrived, he was gone. This and four days of TV dinners were the only things he left behind. Somebody told him to get out, Ari, someone who knew where he was staying." The weightiness of Molly's accusation hung in the air.

"Look, I didn't even know . . ." Ari said, the words tumbling out of her mouth.

Molly's face turned beet red. "Don't!" she shouted. Then, remembering that the patrol officer was in the other room, Molly leaned closer, and whispered, "Don't lie to me." She picked up the card and put it under Ari's nose. "You see how the business phone is crossed out and your cell number is written above it? You've only been unemployed since Tuesday. Now, how would Bob Watson know that unless you'd seen him, or at least talked to him?"

Ari had no answer, and she couldn't lie to Molly anymore. She sighed deeply. "There are things," she began, her eyes filling with tears, "things you do not know about me. Bob . . ."

"Bob?" Molly's harsh whisper rang in Ari's ears. "Bob! What about me? We've made love," Molly said, her voice crumbling at the end. Ari reached for her, tried to put her arms around the detective, but Molly took a step away to regain her composure. In a few seconds she traded hurt for anger. "I just can't believe I was so stupid. Now it all makes sense. You got close to me to learn about the case. That's why you went out with me."

"No," Ari said, shaking her head adamantly. "That's not true."

Molly's face set like stone. "I can't believe anything you say. You knew where he was last night before we slept together. You know my career is on the line here, and you chose to hide this from me." She looked away and laughed. "At least you must have had a little guilty conscience. That's why you didn't want to talk about the case last night. I thought that was odd, considering you'd pumped me for information at every turn. I let it go, because I figured you were genuinely interested in me. God, I was stupid."

Ari brought her hands to her head and sat on the bed. She was shaking all over, unable to believe that everything had fallen apart so quickly.

"I was so stupid to think that a woman like you would ever really be interested in someone like me. As a detective I should know better." Molly stared down at Ari, her eyes focused on the floor. "I just have to know," she said, her voice filled with venom, "did you fake the orgasms?"

The question jolted Ari upright and into Molly's face. "Get out. Unless you're arresting me for something, get out of my house," she said, her index finger pointed at the door.

Molly's natural temperament surfaced. When pushed, she always pushed back. "I'm taking you in for questioning regarding the whereabouts of a prime suspect in a felony."

Ari turned away while Molly watched Ari's shoulders rise and fall with her breathing. Molly swallowed hard, suddenly aware that her mouth was dry and her heart was racing. When Ari faced the detective, her face went hard. "I would like a few minutes to change, please."

Molly glanced at Ari's faded jeans and white T-shirt and nodded, exiting the room. She found Tim Greer leaning against a wall, looking very uncomfortable. He shook his head, but Molly wasn't surprised. Did she really think Bob Watson would be here? She knew why she had stormed into Ari's apartment, and it had very little to do with the case.

Her eyes fell upon the picture of Ari and her father, both of them in uniform. She blinked to hold back tears and closed her eyes. *What the hell is a matter with you, Nelson?* She folded her arms across her chest and steeled herself for Ari's entrance, but her stomach dropped when Ari emerged in a tailored black suit with a red silk blouse. She'd pulled her hair up and put on some makeup. Even with only a few minutes, Ari still looked stunning.

Ignoring Molly, she faced Tim Greer with a slight smile. "I

guess I'm going with you, Tim." Tim nodded and followed Ari out the door, leaving Molly to trail behind.

The three of them were silent during the ride downtown, Molly driving, Tim beside her. At least they hadn't come in a squad car and embarrassed her in front of her neighbors, Ari thought. Molly obviously had some compassion, although the fact that she brought a uniformed officer with her indicated that she had orchestrated the confrontation and intended on questioning Ari from the moment they had knocked on the door. She stared out the window and watched the office buildings whiz by. Once in awhile her eyes drifted to the back of Molly's head and musk filled her nostrils or maybe she was imagining it from this morning when she'd buried her face deep into Molly's curls. Was that really only a few hours ago?

When the precinct's sliding doors opened with a whoosh, Ari was far more prepared for what happened than Molly. The desk sergeant was the first to recognize her, stepping around the counter and kissing both her cheeks. Molly started to say something, but other officers appeared and soon Ari was surrounded by a circle of her father's old friends and a few interested males and females who just wanted to find out what all the commotion was about. Tim Greer joined in the laughter as one of the old timers told a story about Ari and her dad until a sharp glance from Molly pulled him out of the merriment. Ari shifted her stance as the story ended and the laughter died away, more uncomfortable with this little reunion than being questioned about Bob Watson.

"This isn't a social call," Molly snapped, drawing the eyes of the group. "We need to get upstairs." She took Ari's elbow and started to walk away.

The jibes echoed behind them all the way to the elevator: "What are you doing Nelson, arresting her for jaywalking? Must be hard up if you're locking up solid citizens and the daughter of a brother."

If Molly could get any angrier, Ari didn't know how. The

143

detective stalked out of the elevator, her loafers pounding against the tile as she crossed the corridor. Instead of going to an interrogation room, they went to Molly's office, a sight that instantly appalled Ari. Scattered file folder and reports cluttered Molly's desk, along with a bottle of antacid, a half-eaten hamburger still sitting on its greasy wrapper and several vending machine coffee cups. Ari was sure this was her diet for the day. She showed Ari a chair and left, appearing again with a black man who identified himself as her partner, and Captain David Ruskin.

Ari disliked Ruskin intensely. As a rookie, he'd been partnered with her father. After one week on the job, Ruskin found fifty job applications from McDonald's stuffed into his locker and a note urging him to find other employment. Their hatred had continued for another month until Ruskin was reassigned.

"Well, well, if it isn't Ari Adams, our city's favorite daughter," he said, his voice dripping with sarcasm. He perched on Molly's desk facing Ari while Molly sat directly in front of her and Molly's partner huddled in the corner apparently unclear of his role. "So what's the deal, Nelson?"

Molly shifted in her chair, choosing her words carefully. "Ms. Adams's business card was found in Bob Watson's motel room. I'm wondering if she has information about his whereabouts now." Ari noticed she didn't say anything about the scratched out phone number. Her gaze shifted from Molly to Ruskin's smug expression.

"Do you know where Bob Watson is?" he asked.

"No," Ari answered honestly. "I don't have the foggiest."

"But you did," Ruskin continued, "until he packed up and left."

"I don't know where he is," Ari said, avoiding Ruskin's question. Ari glanced at Molly and wondered if she would jump in, but she remained silent, her gaze focused entirely on Ruskin.

"He is one of your best friends, right?" Ruskin asked.

"Yes."

Ruskin hovered over her. "I think you're lying, Ari. I think you know exactly where Bob is and you're protecting him."

"Sorry to disappoint you, David. But as I've already told Detective Nelson, I don't know where Bob is," she said emphatically. It was easy to say because it was the truth.

"Maybe if we kept you here for a little while you might have a change of heart," Ruskin said, a grin pasted on his face.

Molly blanched at the idea of Ari being locked in a cell with some of the women in the Madison jail, even for one minute. "Captain, I'm sure Ari will cooperate."

"I have been cooperating," Ari said curtly. She looked at her watch. "I've been kept here long enough. Either charge me with something and let me call my attorney or I'm leaving." She rose and turned for the door.

Ruskin's voice came from behind her, crawling up her neck like a spider. "Let her go, Nelson. She might have a change of heart and give up the act. You know, Ari, kind of like you being a police officer."

Ari's face darkened. She stepped into Ruskin's physical space. Years before, he'd had it bad for her. She used it to her advantage now, staring at him, letting him smell her perfume and study her lips. He swallowed hard and his eyes wavered. "At least I knew when to get out," she whispered.

Andre suppressed a giggle, but Ruskin shot him a look of contempt. He leaned forward on the desk, his knee grazing her thighs and leered, "You are such a bitch, Adams. That's why you've never had a good man."

Ari smiled and looked down at Ruskin's lap. "David, are we going to discuss all of your shortcomings?"

His face reddened and he started barking obscenities at her, which she returned, until their yelling melded into a loud jumble that Andre and Molly couldn't stop.

"What the hell is going on here?" bellowed Sol Gardner from the doorway. A group of detectives stood behind him, some ready to pull out their weapons. At the sight of the police chief, everyone froze. His stern expression melted at the sight of Ari. He took her by the shoulders and beamed. "Ari, you get lovelier every time I see you. Flannagan tells me that you're being questioned about Bob?"

Ari smiled at her godfather. "Sol, may I speak with you alone?"

The chief nodded and the three other detectives quickly filed out, Ruskin no longer interested since he was outranked. He murmured something to Andre and left. Molly craved a drink and seriously considered disappearing to the corner tavern. She had no idea what Ari was saying to the chief, but he would most likely chew her out for improper procedure.

She'd made a terrible mistake bringing Ari in for questioning. Standing in the apartment, her emotions on overdrive, the words had poured out of her mouth without any logic or thought. She had not been acting as a police officer but as a wounded lover, practically arresting Ari to get even, knowing she would be uncomfortable downtown and that Ruskin would try to make her life miserable, even threaten her. Watching the scenario unfold had been a different story. All of the cops downstairs staring at her like a circus attraction made Molly sick, and then Ruskin threatening Ari with a lockup had sent Molly's gut into spasms.

"Would now be a good time to discuss my follow-up progress?" Andre asked mildly.

"Sure," Molly said, her eyes riveted to the office door.

Andre opened his notes and read. "I still haven't been able to talk to Kristen Duke's roommate, the one who was home when Duke got off work that night." Molly nodded and Andre continued. "She's getting back from San Diego late tomorrow, and I'll talk with her ASAP. I spoke with some more theatre employees and one of them remembers seeing Deborah Thorndike at the end of the movie. Seems she dropped some of her trash onto the

146

floor as she left and the kid who had to clean the theater remembered her simply because he thought she was a bitch."

"Figures," Molly murmured. That sounded like the widow. "I'd say she's probably off the hook." Molly emphasized the probably, never liking to totally eliminate anyone too soon.

"Now here's something interesting. I talked to a few of Lily Watson's table companions at that charity dinner. One of them swears she left the table after dessert and didn't return at all. That would have been around seven thirty. Now she could have been mingling or dancing, or something—"

"Or she could have left and killed Thorndike," Molly interjected.

"Exactly. I'll keep working on that angle. It's possible she moved to another table just to talk to a friend, or that the witness is wrong, since there was an open bar and everyone was drinking." Molly rubbed her temples, envisioning a spider's web, all of the intricate connections and Michael Thorndike at the center. "As for Russ Swanson," Andre continued, "he hasn't been back to his apartment, but there are officers there and at his workplace, so I'm sure we'll pick him up."

"I'll bet you he doesn't know where Watson is now," Molly said. She wondered what Ari and the chief could possibly be discussing for so long.

"Well, his alibi checks out," Andre said. "The judge confirms they were together at the Hilton. Of course this was after he denied the whole thing for half an hour and nearly wet his pants." Molly cracked a smile at the judge's discomfort. "There's something off about Swanson, though," Andre added thoughtfully.

Molly turned her head and looked her partner in the eye, suddenly interested. "What do you mean?"

"I've been looking over Speedy Copy's books, and the pieces don't fit. I can't put my finger on it, but I'll keep looking." Molly knew Andre had minored in finance during college and knew a lot about business. She was happy to let him wade through the bank statements and financial reports, which reminded her that she needed to talk with Cyril Lemond, another person who still had no alibi.

The office door swung open and Sol led Ari toward the elevator. Ari glanced at Molly but her expression was unreadable. Ari didn't seem to be anything—not angry, not upset, just calm. Sol gave her a big hug and held her like a protective father would. Molly found herself aching for Ari, longing to put her own arms around the slight body. Ari had reached for her in the apartment, but she'd been too proud and angry.

The elevator doors closed and Sol motioned to Molly. "In your office, Detective." Molly took a deep breath, preparing herself for the worst—being thrown off the investigation. She sat in her chair before her knees gave out. The chief stood over her, his arms folded across his chest. Molly knew this wouldn't be good.

"As your superior, I'm telling you to rip up any report you started on this little farce, and if you haven't written one, don't start. That young woman is my goddaughter and I doubt she's guilty of anything greater than not telling us where Bob Watson *used* to be."

"But that's a crime," Molly argued.

Sol Gardner made a dismissive gesture. "And in my opinion, forgivable. Do we understand each other?" That was Gardner's way of ending a conversation. He hiked up his pants and leaned over the desk. "Now, as your friend who has slugged down a few beers with you, let me say this: I know Ari. I know a lot *more* about Ari than you do. You're going to need to trust me." He gave her an understanding look before turning to leave. "And I'll tell you one other thing," he said, his hand on the knob, but the door still closed. "I know Bob Watson, and between you and me and the walls, I'm with Ari. I don't think Bob Watson killed Michael Thorndike. You'd be wise to look a little closer at the suspects who haven't flown the coop."

Molly took a breath, the air space increasing with the chief's departure. She sat very still, Gardner's words hitting home, his gut feeling that Watson was innocent. *Her* gut was telling her to finish the bottle of Maalox, which she did in one swig.

Two hours later she slumped back down in her chair and winced. Her ass still hurt from sitting on the poorly padded government issue piece of crap. She looked around. Only her desk light was on, casting shadows into the corners of the small office. When she was here at night, which was often, she'd leave the door open just a crack and do her paperwork in the near dark. She liked sitting in the silence and staring out her window at the city below.

She'd look out into the lights and think about the thousands of people settled into their cozy houses, winding down for the evening. Then she'd think about the violent scum who preyed upon them. Of course, daytime crime stats were almost as bad, but for some reason, it bothered her more to think about the victims of the night.

She didn't want to go home. Although most of the detectives had left and the third floor was quiet, she felt more alone at her apartment, disconnected. The eight hundred square feet she'd inhabited since moving back to Phoenix had merely been an expensive storage unit. The only thing she owned that she loved was the piano. If she went home tonight and found everything gone, she wouldn't care as long as the piano was unharmed.

Depression was a stalker that hounded her relentlessly, kept her on her guard and at times terrified her—like right now. She debated whether or not to call Brian, but the idea slipped away immediately. She knew where she wanted to go.

Vicky the bartender had a whiskey in front of her before she'd planted herself on the stool. Hideaway was just kicking into gear for a Thursday night. She finished the first one and didn't even realize she'd drunk it. With a quick flick of a finger, Vicky poured another shot. Molly was a good tipper and a regular. She got service before most, even if the bar was three deep.

Pity came easy. Why had she ever thought she could have someone like Ari? Or anyone for that matter? She was just too volatile, unable to control her emotions, too unpredictable. Long-term relationships were not for everyone. Some people's personalities demanded that they stay alone, solitary. That was her situation, and after her third shot, she was absolutely convinced that she would die alone.

Loneliness was the emotion she avoided at all cost, sacrificing her common sense and decency at times to escape the feeling. If she really faced the truth, it was what she feared most. Sleeping with strangers provided short-term relief and numbed the pain. She'd convinced herself it was what got her through some hard times.

Her failed relationships were a reaction to loneliness. She'd settled for people who waved red flags in her face that she chose to ignore. Rationalization triumphed. Why wait for someone who might not exist, or if she did, might never cross her path? Take what you can get was her attitude, and Molly had—four times. Four long-term relationships that never should have occurred.

Lost deep in her thoughts, Molly didn't notice the familiar redhead sidle up next to her. Only when the woman's hand massaged her thigh did she look at her. Too much makeup covered her face, but she had a nice mouth. If Molly had one more whiskey, it wouldn't matter.

The redhead increased the pressure of her stroke, and Molly motioned to Vicki.

"Last one," the bartender ordered.

"So you'll be ready to leave after this drink?" the stranger whispered in her ear, her breath smelling of rum and cigarettes. She licked Molly's earlobe tenderly. This was someone who wanted her, who could make the fear disappear or at least force it into the shadows of Molly's heart for awhile, and after today, she was more afraid than ever.

She threw back the whiskey and smacked the glass on the bar. "I'm ready to go now," she announced. Yet, she hesitated. Ari's figure boarding the elevator flashed in her mind. It was gone in a second and only the redhead remained. She buried her tongue deep between the glossy lips, fortifying her resolve.

From across the room, Jane watched Molly and the woman exit the bar.

Chapter Eighteen
Friday, June 22
5:00 a.m.

The blue numbers on the oven's time display flipped to five o'clock, the flicker drawing Molly's attention away from the wall momentarily. The kitchen strained to receive the morning light peeking in from the window, confirming that it was indeed barely dawn. She reclined on the breakfast bar, her legs propped up on the opposite bench. Her back was beginning to ache, but she wanted to feel miserable. She deserved it.

What brought Molly to the crime scene before sunrise was sound advice from her first mentor who believed it was wise to go back to the beginning whenever you felt you were losing your bearings. Molly certainly felt lost, a kite whose string had detached, floating further away from the truth in a direction she couldn't control. Propping her head up with her fists, she closed her eyes and reviewed each piece of evidence and each suspect, her mind turning through the information like cards in a Rolodex. Molly had an amazing memory, one that allowed her to store tiny details in addition to major facts. She sorted it all out as if doing a jigsaw puzzle, connecting like with like and finding a border or frame with which to guide the investigation.

Bob Watson was a critical piece, of this she was sure, but his role was unclear. She shared Sol Gardner's belief that Captain Ruskin was hanging too much on a suspect who kept proving at every turn that he might be innocent, including the test results which confirmed that the gun Andre had taken from Bob's desk had not been fired any time recently.

She wandered into the living room and hovered over the spot where Michael Thorndike was killed. She thought Ari was right about the handwriting. The killer had used Michael Thorndike's hand to write *Robert* on the wall. So then why move him? It was a key question, one she wished she could discuss with Ari.

She gazed out the front window, Ari's red and blue real estate sign barely visible in the soft daylight. Part of the reason she'd come here was to feel close to Ari and get as far away from the previous night as possible. The redhead had been too hung over to notice Molly slipping out of her apartment at three in the morning, Molly herself barely able to operate the truck and bee-line out of the rundown duplex that sat only a block away from Hideaway. She couldn't bring herself to face the woman in daylight, knowing her shame and guilt would be a headline on her forehead. At the same time, she couldn't go home, the loneliness now worse than ever. She had hoped the sex would fill the void in her heart, but it only burned it deeper, and when nightfall came again, she knew she would either be sleeping in her office or at her brother's apartment.

She played the case in her mind for the next two hours as she roamed through the house, periodically stopping and staring into closets, looking out the windows, or sitting on the patio. At seven o' clock a dog walker meandered down the street followed by a schnauzer who just couldn't keep up with its owner's fast stride. They both stopped in front of the house, the dog sniffing the grass border intently, and Molly wondered if the dog could smell the scent of death. The longer the dog sniffed, the more agitated the walker became, trying to coax him along with gentle tugs on the leash. Clad in running clothes, a baseball cap covered his face, and it was only when he looked toward the house that Molly realized it was Cyril Lemond. He looked right at her, and his face paled in recognition. As she came outside to greet him, the schnauzer yipped and growled, his canine senses understanding that his master and the woman approaching were adversaries.

"That's enough, Buddy," Lemond ordered. The schnauzer immediately ceased barking and turned his attention back to an interesting spot on the grass. When Lemond was sure the dog was occupied, he smiled at Molly, the color returning to his face. "Detective Nelson, this is certainly a surprise. I must say I'm impressed that Phoenix's finest seem to be working around the clock to solve Michael's murder." He greeted Molly with a firm handshake, and Molly recoiled slightly at the realization that his hands were softer than her own. "Can I assume that our meeting out here on the street really isn't that coincidental?"

"No, it's not. But I thank you for saving me the extra block," she said, her eyes glancing down the ten houses to Lemond's bungalow. "You certainly live close," Molly added.

His eyes glimmered at her subtle insinuation. "Yes, I was the Watsons' neighbor for three years before they moved. It's a shame something like this happened in this area. The property values will probably plummet now. Probably even more so if it was discovered a murderer lived on the street," he added.

Despite Lemond's attempt to shock her, Molly's face remained neutral and gave no indication of surprise. "Do you know of any murderers who live on this street?" Molly parried.

Lemond grinned. "Actually, no. But you might think so, since

154

I'm the only one of Michael's partners who doesn't have a decent alibi."

"And what was that alibi again?" Molly asked.

Lemond smiled weakly. "I'm afraid it hasn't improved or changed, for that matter, since our first interview. My wife was out of town. I went jogging at six thirty, returned around seven thirty and read a book for the rest of the evening."

"What book?"

"Ironically, *Crime and Punishment*." Molly couldn't help but smile. "Actually," he continued, "I've read it several times. Dostoevsky's conclusions about the human mind are fascinating."

"And they are?" she inquired, curious as to why a potential murder suspect would flaunt an interest in crime.

Lemond blushed. "I'm sorry, Detective. I assumed you were familiar with . . ." he said, his voice trailing off.

"Fiction wasn't covered at the police academy," Molly interjected sharply. Her lack of a college education was a subject she avoided and she always felt inadequate in front of people like Cyril Lemond, even though she knew she shouldn't.

"At any rate, since Buddy can't vouch for me, is it safe to say that I am a suspect?"

Molly hedged. "I think suspect is a strong word. You're more a possibility."

A broad grin spread across Lemond's face. "A possibility. Excellent!"

"You're pleased that we're investigating you?" Molly said slowly.

"Detective, I have nothing to hide, have done nothing wrong, so I'm free to be totally amused by this intriguing foray into my relatively mundane life."

"I wouldn't call a fifty-million-dollar investment mundane, would you?"

Lemond scowled at the mention of the Emporium. "You've

obviously been talking to that idiot, Trainor, Thorndike's little minion. If Michael had told Felix the sky was purple, Felix would have asked what shade."

"So, then you didn't like Michael's plans for the Emporium?"

Lemond jerked on Buddy's leash. "Pipe dream. Michael was a great developer, but I think he was losing his touch."

"Felix Trainor didn't think so," Molly countered.

Lemond glanced at her. "There were rumors, you know."

"About what?"

"Them."

Molly shrugged. She remembered what Trainor had said about the gossip, and now she was sure she knew the source. "I take it you don't like Felix Trainor?"

Lemond sighed. "Michael brought Felix in two years ago as some sort of visionary. He proved very helpful in the development of the sports arena. However, since its completion, he's really been very worthless."

"So are you and Mrs. Denman looking to fire Mr. Trainor?"

Lemond's eyes danced. He knew what Molly was thinking. With Michael Thorndike dead, it would be easier to edge Trainor out. "Partners cannot be fired, Detective, they have to resign on their own accord. However," he added with a cruel smile, "if life becomes unpleasant for Felix, he may very well do that."

"You seem to enjoy that idea, Mr. Lemond," Molly observed.

Lemond stared at his dog, whose nose was buried in a thicket of grass. "Let's just say, it would be an added bonus to Michael's death."

"You mean in addition to the fifty-million-dollar savings, don't you? Lose two partners instead of one, avoid an unwise business deal that would make you cash poor, and finally, become chairman of the League, right?" Molly paused and stared at Lemond. His gray eyes narrowed at her insinuations. "Sounds to me like there were many bonuses for you if Michael Thorndike was gone."

"I think it's time I got back to the house. If you have any further questions for me, please direct them to my attorney." He gave Buddy's leash a vicious tug, the small dog springing next to him, and started to walk away.

"Mr. Lemond, may I ask you one more question?" Molly called.

He turned and faced her.

"How does the book end?"

He looked confused for a second, but then looked away. "The main character, Raskalnakov, confesses."

"Somehow I don't think that will happen in this case," Molly said sarcastically. "Do you?"

He glared at her. "I have no idea." He stalked off, the schnauzer galloping next to him.

Chapter Nineteen
Friday, June 22
12:16 p.m.

Thinking was the real enemy but Ari decided to declare war on dirt instead. She'd been in combat since five in the morning when she woke up and gathered the cleaning supplies, starting in the furthest corner of her bedroom and methodically working inch by inch through the whole condo. Every crevice was wiped and scrubbed, including the places most people avoided until their next move. And Ari wasn't simply wiping things off with a shrug. Her muscles throbbed after six hours of applying elbow grease to spots and stains that outdated her lease and her back ached from scrunching over the baseboards armed with her old toothbrushes.

It was then, with sweat pouring off her T-shirt, that Ari

thought of the Michael Thorndike murder, the crime scene and the floor. There was still something bothering her . . .

The phone rang for the third time, the first two were hang-ups and Ari wondered if Molly was calling, but Jane's voice followed the beep, urging Ari to call. Ari paused, her scrub brush poised over the soap ring that lined the inside of the tub. Jane sounded strange, which was unusual for someone who spent her life on the phone and could talk calmly to a client even in the midst of a terrorist invasion. Ari willed herself to finish the tub, the last unclean area of her whole apartment, before her energy depleted entirely.

Twenty minutes later, propped up against the side of the tub, arms at her side, scrub brush discarded a few feet away, Ari took some deep breaths and allowed fatigue to paralyze her body. Since her muscles were no longer engaged in activity, the wheels of her mind, shut down during the cleaning frenzy, began to turn. That was one thing about Ari—she was constantly in motion, either physically or mentally.

It was impossible not to think of Molly and the horrible betrayal she must feel. She had promised Molly she would alert her if Bob called and she had not done that. She had followed Bob to his motel room and never once reached for her cell phone to summon the police. But worst of all, the thought that tied Ari's stomach into knots was the fact that she had chosen a friend over her lover. She never should have gone to bed with Molly while the case was being investigated—that was her big mistake. Stuck in the middle between Bob and Molly was an unenviable position and inevitably she was forced to choose. The only thing that could be worse than losing Molly would be learning that Bob was in fact guilty and she had chosen incorrectly.

The doorbell rang, and only after it was obvious the ringer wasn't leaving, did Ari hoist herself from the floor and hobble to the door. Jane stood at the threshold, a bag from Freddy's Deli dangling from one arm and a quart of double fudge ripple ice cream in the crook of the other.

"How did you know I was in crisis?" Ari asked, her rubber gloved hands on her hips.

"Good guess," Jane replied, sailing past Ari and the truth. She prepared plates while Ari retreated to her immaculate shower and scrubbed the first two layers of cleaners from her skin. When she returned, Jane was sitting at the dining room table, her hands folded in her lap, a brisket of beef sandwich in front of her. Ari noticed a duplicate sandwich on an adjoining plate, and while she couldn't look at the food, the smell intrigued her and her stomach started to rethink its position.

"Why didn't you answer your phone?" Jane asked, lifting her sandwich with her well manicured fingers.

"I was busy."

"So was I," Jane said. "I was getting to know a potential client." Ari raised an eyebrow. She knew Jane's tactics. "We were exchanging phone numbers," she continued. Ari rolled her eyes. "Well, phone numbers and a few bodily fluids," Jane admitted. She had a Cheshire cat grin on her face. She was trying to shock Ari, who just chewed on her pickle spear in response.

Nothing Jane said or did surprised her any longer. At the Melissa Etheridge concert last year, she'd taken off her shirt, thrown it on the stage and continued dancing topless for the rest of the show. Jane was a wild child and lived totally for the moment. It was hard to believe *that* woman was the same woman who sat across from Ari now, dabbing mayo daintily from the corners of her painted lips so as not to smudge her makeup.

She read Ari's thoughts. "What?"

Ari laughed and covered her mouth with her hand. "I just can't believe you're you."

Jane smiled broadly and preened. "I'm one of a kind, babe, and don't you forget it." The conversation waned, Ari still concerned about Jane. Something was clearly bothering her but she obviously had no desire to talk about it.

As usual, Ari finished first while Jane, who ate like a cotillion graduate, speared bite size pieces of her sandwich with a fork, not allowing a single crumb to fall in her lap.

"So, have you spoken to Molly?" Jane asked.

"No, and I doubt I will. It's over," Ari said sullenly, desperately hoping the words weren't true.

"Maybe that's for the best," Jane commented.

"I thought you liked Molly," Ari said, surprised at Jane's defeatist attitude. Usually Jane was a champion of love, especially hopeless love.

"I do like her," Jane said quickly. She paused and finished the last bite of sandwich while Ari waited. "But she did a rotten thing."

Ari shrugged. "I would have done the same. I lied to her, Jane, and what's worse is that I spent an entire evening with her and didn't tell her. There were about four times when I knew I should say something, but I never did. She hates me, and I can't blame her."

Jane folded her napkin in fourths and set it on her plate all the while watching Ari's pained expression. This was Ari. Perfect Ari. If her behavior was even slightly questionable, she blamed herself for everything and forgave everyone else. In her own mind, her conduct had to be above reproach or everyone else's mistakes were excusable. She set standards for herself most people never would, and if they did, they would fall terribly short of achieving them, like a high jumper who could never get over the bar.

Jane certainly could never live up to Ari's standards and she doubted Molly could either, so she chose to remain silent about Molly's indiscretion. Although Ari was her best friend, she felt a kinship with Molly that Ari would never understand. Staring at the detective from across the bar, Jane had recognized the lost expression, one she had seen in the mirror many times.

"Any more thoughts on the case?" Jane asked.

Ari shrugged, uninterested in anything but her own problems. She was furious with Bob for putting her in this position. "Jane, at this point, if Bob's too stupid to stop running from the police, he deserves everything that happens to him. Let his little mistress deal with it."

Jane read Ari's face. She acted like she didn't care but inside, Jane knew Ari was in turmoil. A thought occurred to her. "Ari, are you sure Bob and Kristen were working that night? I mean, maybe they were at some hotel, and Bob just doesn't want to say anything at the risk of having his illicit love affair revealed."

"Jane, that's a little farfetched. Bob said they were working."

Jane made a dismissive gesture and snorted. "I guess it depends on how you define work."

Ari shook her cup and sipped the last of her drink. "Their affair explains a lot. Both of them were very strange when I talked to them. Kristen hinted around at it throughout the whole conversation. I suspected there was something going on, but I really wasn't sure enough to say anything."

"Obviously Lily doesn't know or Bob would have been up front from the beginning. I mean, I think she'd probably freak out. I only met her once, but that woman's got a temper. Great nails, too, but definitely a hothead." Jane examined her own manicure and flicked an invisible speck of dirt away.

"I don't think Lily suspects anything. She assumes Bob is totally devoted to her."

"You know, if this proves Bob's innocent, then why was his name on the wall?" Ari shook her head. That was the question she had been unable to answer all along. "Maybe someone was out to get Bob and killing Thorndike was just a way to do it," Jane theorized.

That was a pretty long stretch, but there was something about that idea that struck a chord. She just couldn't put her finger on it. She opened her mouth to discuss it with Jane, when the phone rang.

She had barely said hello when Bob's voice boomed over the line, loud enough for Jane to mouth his name. Ari nodded her assent and tried to focus on Bob's words, which were coming out so fast she couldn't understand him. "Bob! Slow down, and start over. What are you trying to tell me?"

"Ari, they arrested Russ this morning!"

"What?"

"They arrested Russ this morning for embezzlement, and they're rechecking his alibi for the night of Thorndike's murder."

"They think Russ killed Michael Thorndike?" Ari asked for Jane's benefit. Jane shook her head and rolled her eyes.

"They're not sure about that. What they are sure about is that he bribed Michael Thorndike! That's how we got the Speedy Copy location downtown. I'd met with my banker a few times, trying to figure out what the hell Russ was doing to the books. I didn't want to confront him until I had proof, but apparently, he confessed to it today. Said he had bribed Thorndike but he didn't kill him."

"So you had no idea Russ paid off Michael Thorndike?" she interjected.

"No," Bob said, his voice cracking. "At least the bastard told them that. He said I didn't have anything to do with it, and I didn't, Ari, I really didn't." She could tell the last part was said for her benefit. "I mean, I was surprised that we got the location, but I figured we won the bid fair and square. Michael Thorndike may be powerful, but he's one man. He was only one vote on the committee. I thought they'd been bowled over by our presentation. I never thought there were any tricks, and I certainly didn't think my partner was making a shady deal behind my back."

Bob's gum smacked in Ari's ear. She was sure he was furious and if Russ ever did get out of prison, she worried about what Bob would do to him. "This is going to hit the newspapers today," he continued. "It's gonna kill my reputation, this combined with the murder investigation."

"Not necessarily," Ari said. "Russ claims you didn't know and if there's nothing that can tie you to it—"

163

"There's nothing," he shot back. "This was all him, the little prick."

Ari heard him breathing deeply. She sensed he was starting to calm down, his emotions vented. Now was the time for logic. "Bob, please come back. You need to be here to defend your business."

"Not yet, Ari. There's still a murderer out there who's willing to let me go to prison."

"Do you know who it is?" Bob didn't say anything for several seconds, long enough for Ari to gauge that he was calling from a payphone at a busy intersection. "You do, don't you? You know who killed Michael Thorndike." It was no longer a question but a statement.

"Yes," came the simple reply. Before Ari could ask questions or protest, the traffic noise disappeared, and only when the annoying dial tone echoed in her ear, did she hang up.

Chapter Twenty
Friday, June 22
5:53 p.m.

Molly left the city for the rural outskirts, the street numbers hitting triple digits. Her parents lived in Avondale, a community that possessed as many sorghum fields as it did housing developments. Caught in their version of David and Goliath, the farmers fought to keep their heritage, but each year there were fewer and fewer blocks of green and brown, and they watched the houses encroach their territory a little more. Goliath was clearly going to win this one.

She drove through one of the many developments that bordered the highway, tract homes that all looked alike—beige stucco and tile roofs. Molly's father was a semi-retired plumber who owned his own small company. A white truck sat in the driveway, Nelson Plumbing painted on the side. As she wandered inside, her ears were assaulted by screaming children. Her niece, Chelsey, a honey blond five year old, raced around her, eagerly pursued by Kenny, Chelsey's three-year-old brother.

Molly followed the peals of laughter down the narrow hallway into the kitchen, which was the hub of activity. Her sister-in-law, Jenna, a petite brunette with a serious expression intercepted the children, while her brother, Don Jr., set the table. She watched the commotion, glad to be home, away from the city and its problems, and more importantly, away from her own.

"Hey, sis," he called, distributing the plates. Jenna smiled as she passed by Molly, one child under each arm.

The greeting got the attention of Molly's parents, who were standing in the kitchen working on dinner. Her mother wiped her hands on a dish towel and rushed to give Molly a ferocious hug. Her equal in height, with the legs of a dancer, Teddy Nelson stared into her daughter's eyes, a worried expression forming on her face. "What's wrong?"

Unwilling to dampen the evening with her multitude of problems, she shook her head and turned to her father, who had joined his wife.

"Hey, honey," her father, the elder Don, said warmly. Not only did Molly sound like her father, she looked like him too. God had played a little prank on the only Nelson daughter, giving Molly her father's strong jaw and body, while her brother, Fred, got the tall, lean figure from his mother. Molly had long forgiven him and God for the mix-up, figuring Fred had used the gift better than she ever would, having won two state swim championships with his lanky frame.

Don broke the silence with a drink request, and once she was armed with a Budweiser, Molly allowed herself to wander around the house, trying to forget that Ari was supposed to have come with her. She imagined if Ari were there, she would have given her a tour of the house, and Ari would have gawked at all the photos of Molly that adorned the walls, bookcases, dressers and nightstands of each room. Molly in her baptismal dress, her

Little League pictures, a grinning cowgirl at Halloween, her first flying lesson and her senior portrait. Interspersed were photos of her four brothers. Besides Fred and Don, there was Gary, a rodeo clown, and Brian.

Circling back into the kitchen ended her peaceful moments and thrust her into the family chaos. Chelsey and Kenny laughed heartily at the blaring TV, while father and son debated the Phoenix Suns' season. Jenna enlisted Molly's help with the salad, and soon she really had forgotten everything that weighed on her mind.

When they sat down half an hour later, one seat was empty since Brian was still working on his last plumbing call. The room turned pleasantly silent, everyone devouring Teddy's fabulous dinner. Molly ignored her arteries' cry for mercy and filled her plate with fried chicken and dumplings. In between bites, her family conducted a tag-team debate about political and social issues. The Nelsons were up on current events, and everyone participated in the discussion. There were no introverts allowed.

The squeak of the screen door brought a pause to the conversation as Brian Nelson shuffled through the kitchen and headed straight for the laundry room, his work boots clunking against the tile. When he joined them at the table, he leaned over and kissed his only sister on the cheek. "Hey, Mol. Catch any bad guys?"

Molly fiddled with the gold hoop that dangled from his left ear. Except for the twinkling blue eyes and winning smile, he was a stark contrast to the rest of his family. His waist-length blond hair was tied back in a ponytail, and his tank top exposed the many tattoos that covered his biceps and forearms. He wouldn't win any awards for Mr. All-American, but his magnetic personality had always attracted the girls. Molly loved all her brothers, but Brian was special.

"Where's Lynne?" Molly asked, surprised that Brian's steady girlfriend was absent.

"She had a study group," Brian answered between bites.

Molly nodded, knowing that this was Lynne's final year of her architectural program. It amazed her family that Brian, the family scamp, had landed such a classy woman as Lynne.

"Did Mrs. Polanski's shower turn out okay?" Don inquired of his son.

Brian picked up the bowl of dumplings and frowned. "I'll finish tomorrow," he said evenly.

"You didn't finish today?" his father asked incredulously. "That's a one-day job. You should have finished." Brian assaulted his dinner, spearing his food angrily. "Can't keep doing one-day jobs in two," his father continued. "You'll drive us out of business." Brian ate like a maniac, his jaws pulverizing whatever was inside. Molly watched the exchange between the two of them, knowing the outcome before it happened. "So what was the holdup?" Don demanded.

Brian's answer came through clenched teeth. "There was a problem. It would have taken you twice as long too."

The challenge in his voice was clear. Molly focused on her beer. Don Junior and Jenna pretended to discipline the children. Only Teddy showed any reaction, patting her husband's hand to calm him down.

"How's business?" Molly offered, hoping to avoid a confrontation. Brian welcomed the diversion and opened his mouth to respond, but Don quickly cut him off. "Won't be a business much longer."

It was too much. Brian dropped his napkin on the table and stomped outside. Molly fought the urge to jump up and follow Brian out, knowing that it would ruin the evening for everyone else. Brian's clashes with their father dated back to childhood, and everyone in the family had learned not to take sides, but just stay out of the way.

The atmosphere lightened with Brian's departure, Don returning to his jovial self, the encounter forgotten like a black cloud that rolled away.

After dinner, when she was sure that her father was planted in front of ESPN, Molly made a huge plate of food and carried it to the back shed, Brian's refuge from the world and the home of his prized possession—an Aston Martin he was slowly restoring. She found him under the car, two feet in heavy work boots keeping time to music that Molly couldn't hear. She kicked the left one and waited for Brian to roll out on the dolly. He took off his Walkman and faced her. "Sorry," was all he said.

Molly gave a sympathetic smile and motioned to the plate while she retrieved two beers from a small refrigerator and they settled down at his workbench. "The car's coming along," Molly commented, noticing that most of the body work was done.

"Got about another year I figure," Brian said between bites. Molly slugged down the rest of her beer and went for another. With his eyes focused on his dinner he asked, "How much you drinkin'?"

Molly inhaled. Only her favorite brother could ask that question and get a true answer and not a fist in his jaw. "You don't want to know," she said frankly. "I'm on a killer case, I hate my life and I'm seriously considering turning straight." Brian blinked in shock. "Okay, that's not true," Molly admitted, "but my life sucks." She put her head down on the workbench and cried.

His hands covered in grease, Brian resisted the urge to smooth her hair. She'd probably been holding it in for days. Molly was not a crier. When her sobs had faded, he leaned over and kissed the top of her head. "A dollar for your thoughts," he said.

Molly couldn't help but crack a small smile as Brian resorted to the saying of their childhood created during the recession of the Seventies. She had offered a penny for his thoughts one day when he was six. He said that with inflation, she'd need at least a dollar. The phrase had stuck long after the era had ended. She poured her heart out to Brian, starting with Michael Thorndike's murder, her intense attraction to Ari and finally her encounter with the redhead from the bar.

"Why do you think you did that?" he asked nonjudgmentally.

"You mean why did I have a meaningless sexual encounter with someone I just met?" When he didn't respond, she sighed. "You know what I don't get is that I feel like I cheated on Ari. We've known each other a few days, we've only slept together once, so why the hell do I feel so guilty?"

"You tell me," Brian responded, already knowing the answer.

Molly stared back at her brother. She knew the answer too.

"Why don't you stay at my place for a few days," Brian offered. "I think you need a break from your own life. How long has it been since you've flown a plane?"

Molly shook her head, unable to remember the last time she'd sat in a cockpit or actually done anything fun on a weekend.

"That's it, then," Brian concluded.

Before Molly could thank him, her mother appeared at the shed door, the cordless phone in her hand. "Molly, honey, it's your partner."

Molly had to tell Andre to speak up twice before she could understand what he was saying. "We've got a situation," she heard through the crackle of static.

"What's going on?" she asked.

"Deborah Thorndike called. She was going through Michael's papers and found something very interesting, something she thought we would want to see."

"What?" she repeated as she headed toward her parents' house and better reception.

"It turns out Michael Thorndike kept a journal or a notebook of some sort. Deborah never knew it existed, but it's got all of his thoughts and stuff. It's really strange, Molly. It's like he had to brainstorm everything before he made a decision. Had to write it down. He's got flowcharts and notes and pro and con lists. The man was totally organized."

Molly pulled open the back door and shut it behind her before she asked the obvious question. "He didn't happen to mention the name of someone who might want to kill him?"

"Almost," Andre said, his voice filled with glee. "Apparently, he decided to break up with his mistress two days before he was killed. Wrote out a whole list of reasons why he couldn't continue the relationship. I'd say we'd better have a chat with Lily Watson again."

Chapter Twenty-one
Saturday, June 23
8:47 a.m.

Ari cleared off her dining room table as she tried to clear her thoughts of Michael Thorndike's murder and Molly. She hadn't slept more than two hours, her mind unable to stop working, her heart filled with remorse and guilt. There was no way her body would let her rest; it seemed the only way to avoid total depression was to keep moving. She was forced to torture herself and continue the spring cleaning from the day before, only today would be her professional life. She would sort through every file and paper she owned, alphabetize everything and organize it all properly. In the end, she might drop dead of exhaustion, but her body would hit a sparkling floor and Jane could find her last will and testament easily.

She started with her most recent files. The oak table was quickly covered in a sea of white. Real estate agents were paper

172

pushers just like attorneys, and she had more than most because of the extra notes she took. Jane called them "Ari's anals," a crude term that always made Ari scowl whenever Jane said it. They did, however, indicate the level of thoroughness with which she handled any transaction. She kept a running record of every phone conversation, interview or initial meeting with a client. You just never knew what would be important later.

She picked up Bob Watson's file and started sorting through it. She read her notes from their initial meeting eight months ago, where Bob and Lily told her why his parents were selling, where the house was and other real estate related details.

Her mind went back to that time and she pulled the memories from her subconscious. Signing the listing, walking through the house with Bob—still taking meticulous notes and fighting with him about the flooring. He had insisted on dealing with the floor guy and supervising the placement of the oak planks. Why was that? There was some little detail, some reason . . .

The doorbell rang, squashing the burgeoning thought. Ari could already hear Jane's voice speaking to another person. She opened the door to discover Jane, alone and arguing with someone on her cell phone. Jane wandered through the open door and headed straight for the couch. From the bits and pieces she could gather, Ari knew Jane was talking to another agent, probably one on the other side of a deal judging from her combative tone. She went to the kitchen and poured some iced tea, and by the time she returned, Jane was using her standard exit lines, trying to end the call. It took three times, but finally she snapped the phone shut and dropped it in her bag.

"Why is it every agent I deal with has an IQ smaller than his shoe size?" Ari smiled at the sentiment. She'd had her own share of agents who entered the profession only because it was a quick way to get into a career. Three weeks and a person could have the same legal power as an attorney—the ability to write contracts.

Ari shrugged and handed her friend the tea. Jane noticed the stacks of files and papers on Ari's dining room table. "What, are you quitting?" she joked.

"Doubtful," Ari replied. "My career seems to be the highlight of my life." She sat in front of the Watson file and willed the previous thought back into her mind. She'd been so close to retrieving it. "Why would you move a body?" she asked out loud.

"To cover something up," Jane answered from the couch.

"Possibly. But Thorndike was just lying in the middle of the floor. There was nothing there," Ari said.

"Well, then," Jane countered, "if you're not covering something up, you're uncovering it." Ari nodded at the simple logic.

"Or the killer just needed his body out of the way to write the name," Jane added as an afterthought.

He needed him out of the way. The niggle finally broke the surface. Ari sifted through her notes, looking for the ones she took when she and Bob had discussed the floor. She found the sheets and scanned her scribbles, the fragmented words and symbols that no one else would understand. Grabbing the phone, she punched in Bob's number.

"What are you doing?" Jane asked, stretched out on the couch and reading a fashion magazine.

"Solving a mystery," Ari answered. When Bob's voice mail picked up, she disconnected and punched in the number of the Tempe store while she checked her watch. It was still early, but maybe Kristen would know where Bob was, if she'd answer the phone.

"Hello?" Kristen sounded far away and Ari could barely hear her.

"Kristen, it's Ari Adams, Bob's friend. I wanted to know if you'd heard from him."

"No. He hasn't called," she said, a little too quickly.

"Kristen, look, I know about your affair, and I want to help Bob too. I just need to talk to him. If he calls you, please have him call me as soon as possible. I've got some questions about his parents' house." When Kristen, didn't answer, Ari thought she'd hung up. "Kristen?"

"Yeah, I'm still here. He's supposed to call pretty soon."

"Well, when he does, tell him to call me on my cell phone. I'm going to check something out, but I'll have it with me. Okay?"

Ari heard a long pause before Kristen said, "I'll tell him," and then she disconnected abruptly.

Ari grabbed her bag and Bob's file and headed for the door.

"Ari, what's going on in your head?" Jane called, but Ari had already left.

Chapter Twenty-two
Saturday, June 23
2:35 p.m.

Ari didn't even bother to park the SUV properly as she pulled up to the house. All the possible scenarios played through her head. Perhaps Lily and Michael Thorndike were still seeing each other and Bob found out. Would his love for Kristen be enough to forgive Lily a second affair? She wondered if Bob had lied to her about his friendly conversation with Michael Thorndike.

As she worked the lockbox and inserted the front door key, she hesitated. After what happened last time, knowing she was anywhere near this house alone would give Molly cause to freak out, but then again, the detective probably wouldn't care now. She regretted not telling Jane where she was going. She looked up and down the street. It was just another weekend, eerily similar to the past Sunday when everything began. She took a deep breath and stepped across the threshold.

She quickly opened the blinds, sunlight pouring into the living room. She walked behind the bar, *Robert* still splayed on the wall in dried blood. The wall wasn't really the focus of interest, although someone had wanted it to be.

She stared at the small space between the bar and the wall. During her initial tour with Bob, he'd made many side comments about the house, and one of them had to do with the floor—and the safe. She'd absently written down the word in her notes and had forgotten about it when Bob said it wasn't functional and he intended to cover it permanently. Ari knew it couldn't be included in the listing. Since he'd handled the entire floor installation, she'd had no reason to think of it again.

She squatted down, thoroughly uncomfortable with the bloody wall two inches away, not to mention the fact that she had been in this position when she was attacked before. At first glance, there didn't seem to be anything unusual about the planks. She tried to wiggle them but they didn't move. She shone the flashlight up and down the seams caked with Michael Thorndike's blood.

Nothing unusual. Perhaps her hunch was wrong.

She checked along the baseboard, back and forth. During the second pass, she glimpsed a small notch in the center. She inserted the blade of her pocketknife and was amazed when the entire baseboard popped off with a simple tug.

She closed the pocketknife and stuffed it into her shorts. Her attention was riveted to the planks. With a firm grip, she pulled the plank forward. An entire section came forward with great difficulty. She paused, took another breath and using both hands and all her strength, she tugged mightily. It gave suddenly, sending Ari backward a few feet.

She crawled back to the exposed space and stared at the dial of a safe. She pulled at the handle and the door swung open freely, its lock inoperable. Ari stared at the small caliber gun and was sure she had found the murder weapon in a place only her best friend knew existed.

Bob, the one who had insisted on personally supervising the floor installation, shutting Ari out of the loop, probably forgetting the offhanded remark he'd made about his dad's secret place to stash his valuables. Suddenly she felt very foolish for ever having believed him.

A shadow crossed in front of her and Ari turned around.

Molly pulled off her jacket and faced Lily Watson. The woman had said nothing for the first hour, not a single word. It had taken that long to pull her attorney out of the Diamondbacks game and get him to the station. All the while Lily had stared at Molly, contempt pouring out of her. When Arthur Primrose had finally arrived, clad in a D-backs jersey and cap, he requested another hour to conference with his client. Now, two hours later, Molly was hot, impatient and very angry herself. She matched Lily's seething gaze with her own.

"My client is willing to answer any questions you have, Detective Nelson," Primrose announced cheerily. His mood was in sharp comparison to that of his client's, who gave him a cold stare.

"I said I would answer any *new* questions, Arthur. Detective Nelson is the master of the broken record, asking the same things over and over. So you have anything new, Detective?" Lily asked, her voice dripping in sarcasm.

"Did you know Michael Thorndike wasn't going to leave his wife?" Molly shot the question at Lily hoping to catch her off guard.

It seemed to have the opposite effect, since she cocked her head to one side and grinned. "Yes, I knew that." Molly paused, stunned by Lily's demeanor and certain she was missing something. The hinges on the interrogation room's door squeaked as Andre appeared, drawing the attention of all three of them.

He looked green. "Molly, I need to see you. Now." He disappeared and Molly followed him out, grateful for the break and an opportunity to regroup her thoughts. Andre was slumped in a chair, chewing on a nail. "I think I screwed up," he stated simply.

"What do you mean?"

"I finally interviewed Kristen Duke's other roommate this morning. You know, the one who can verify her alibi?"

Molly nodded, her gut already starting to turn. "Yeah."

"She wasn't there. That whole story about her and Kristen watching a movie was bogus. She never saw Kristen. It seems she went on a spur-of-the-moment camping trip with her boyfriend that afternoon. She says she left a note with directions, but Kristen never mentioned it to me. I couldn't find her for three days, and I went along thinking Kristen had an alibi."

"Which may have been exactly what she wanted." Molly sighed deeply. "Where is Kristen now?"

"That's the other part. She's supposed to be at work, but she never showed up. I'm gonna get right on it," he added.

"Great," Molly said. She stared at the interrogation room door, knowing she would once again have to face Lily Watson. "You're right, Andre," she agreed. "You really screwed up."

"You haven't figured much out, have you?" Kristen asked. Ari quickly noticed the thirty-eight she held in her hand. "Why don't you stand up?"

Ari closed the door to the safe and slowly rose against the wall. Kristen's eyes drifted to the bulge in her pocket. She casually walked over and took the gun from Ari's jacket, throwing it so hard it skidded down the hallway.

"How did you get here? I thought you were at the Tempe store."

With her free hand, Kristen pulled out her cell phone from the depths of her jacket pocket. "Call forwarding. Isn't technology wonderful?"

"Terrific," Ari responded.

"You thought it was Bob, right?" she said, her tone smug.

"Or Lily," Ari admitted. "I didn't think anyone else knew about the safe."

"Who do you think ordered the floor? His trusted assistant."

"Who also happened to be his lover," Ari added.

"Believe me, our relationship was all in his head," she stated bluntly.

"So you weren't lovers?"

She sighed, and Ari noticed she tended to look away when she spoke. "We fucked. Bob had this romantic notion that we were in love, but it was all him. I already had a man."

The truth slapped Ari in the face. "Michael Thorndike."

Kristen grinned. "Now you're catching on. Do you want to know the sordid details?" Ari nodded. "We met when Russ Swanson sent me over to Michael's office with some documents. I didn't even know who Michael Thorndike was, but he put the moves on me during the first five minutes. It was the beginning of something special."

Kristen's eyes drifted away, and Ari used the opportunity to remove the knife from her pocket. "I'm lost," she announced. "How did you wind up with Bob?"

"It was Michael's idea. Brilliant, really. When I mentioned that I thought Bob had a crush on me, he decided to use it to his advantage. This was right around the time Russ and Bob were negotiating for the downtown store." Lost in her own story, she didn't notice Ari's hand slide behind her back.

"So you were Michael's spy?" Ari was dumbfounded. She hadn't given Kristen enough credit.

"A regular Mata Hari," Kristen said proudly. "I was the one who suggested to Michael that he could take a bribe from Russ Swanson. Russ has no spine." Kristen leaned against the bar. She was holding the gun like a cocktail drink, not even aware that it wasn't pointed anywhere near Ari.

180

"That makes you a conspirator and a spy, correct?"

"Don't forget murderess."

"How did you do it?"

Kristen smiled. "When I told you a fax came in that night at the store, that wasn't a lie. There was a fax, but it was for me from Michael. I'd asked him to meet me, because I wanted to discuss our situation."

Ari watched Kristen fidget with the gun. She was becoming more agitated and impatient. "And what was your situation?"

"He'd dumped me two days before. It was that bitch, his wife. He was going to leave her, but then she threatened to take half of everything. Once the asshole broke out the calculator and realized how much he was going to lose, he told me he couldn't *afford* to get a divorce." Kristen's voice trembled along with her body. "I loved him, that bastard. I'd given up everything for him."

"And you couldn't let him get away with that."

"Of course not! He said we could keep having fun together, but that's not what I wanted."

"You wanted it all."

Tears welled in Kristen's eyes and she nodded. Ari could sense she wasn't on guard and Ari knew she would need to act quickly. She took a step closer to Kristen and gripped the knife tightly.

"Why did you come here?"

"It was vacant. I figured it would be a few days before anyone suspected. So, I got here first. I pried open the back door and met him when he rang the bell. He tried to reason with me, make excuses, lie. But there was nothing he could say at that point."

"Where'd the gun come from?"

"I always keep a gun in my purse," she answered. "Anybody who works nights should always have a gun."

Ari was running out of questions and options. She needed to distract Kristen. "So where did *that* gun come from?" she asked, motioning to the one Kristen held in her hand.

181

"This one? The one I'm going to kill you with?" Ari nodded. "This is a recent purchase, and of course, you already discovered the murder weapon." They both looked at the safe beneath Ari.

"What I don't understand," Ari said slowly, "is why you hid the gun in the safe. Why not throw it out?"

Kristen shook her head. "My father owned that gun. It's sentimental to me. I needed it to disappear for awhile, but I figured that once Bob was arrested and time had passed, I'd break into the house again and take it back. Who would know? Besides it's not like there's a bunch of lakes and rivers in Phoenix that you can toss a gun into," she added sarcastically.

Kristen took a few steps away from the bar and said, "It's strange how we keep meeting this way. You interrupted me the other night when I came back." She laughed and rolled her eyes. "Stupid me. I forgot to wipe the handle." She stared at Ari. "I was certainly surprised to see you. I could have killed you, you know. But I didn't want to. I liked you."

"Is that going to stop you from killing me now?" Ari asked.

Kristen frowned. "It's really your own fault. If you'd just stayed out of it."

"So why did you write Bob's name on the wall?"

Kristen came closer. Ari knew she would only have one opportunity. "Now, I know you've figured that out. Why don't you tell me?"

"To throw the police off. You wrote the name Robert because you thought Michael probably called him by his full name since they were business associates. And after you wrote Bob's name in blood with Thorndike's hand, you dragged his body into the living room. You figured that would keep them from noticing the safe."

"And it did. Not even Bob thought about it. He told me to have the floor guy cover it up, and I'm sure he thought his precious lover did exactly as she was told." Kristen closed her mouth and stared at Ari. Question and answer time was over. She

182

approached Ari, the gun squarely aimed at her chest. "You know, I've always wondered what it would be like to be with a woman."

"It's better than being with a man," Ari said. "Women know what women need. They know each other's secrets," she whispered. As Ari hoped she would, Kristen blushed at Ari's flirtation and looked away. Ari saw her chance. She lunged forward, throwing Kristen off balance and thrusting the knife forward at the same time. Kristen shifted her weight and Ari's stab glanced her shoulder, the blade barely penetrating the skin.

Still, it was enough to make her cry out and step back. Ari pushed away and lunged toward the hall and the discarded gun, but Kristen tripped her and sent her sprawling. She rolled into the middle of the floor while Kristen screamed as she watched her shoulder bleed. "Bitch!" she yelled.

Ari found her feet and ran toward the hallway when a shot penetrated the air. Then Ari wasn't standing anymore. She moved her head from side to side, looking first at the living room and then the kitchen. She was going to die not twenty feet from where she'd discovered Michael Thorndike's body just one week before.

Kristen stood over her, a look of superiority on her face. "Okay, that just pissed me off," she said calmly, wincing as she touched her shoulder. "And from where I'm standing, I'd say my shoulder looks a lot better than yours."

Only then did Ari feel the throbbing. Pain flooded through her body, and she was dizzy. Her eyes darted around the room. She was helpless.

Kristen smiled. "No way out, Ari. Or, maybe I should put it in terms you'll understand. This sale is final."

Ari watched Kristen point the gun at her and fire.

She imagined herself drifting away, darkness nearby, reaching out to her. She managed to focus long enough to watch Kristen fall backward, the gun still in her hand. But how could that have happened? How could she be watching? She was a murder victim, shot at close range. The sound of quick feet penetrated the ringing in her ears from the gun's blasts.

"Ari, honey," a voice called. Someone was standing over her, holding her gun at his side. The voice materialized into Bob, looming over her, his face full of concern. Somehow the situation seemed familiar, and she was filled with déjà vu. "Sweetie, it's going to be okay," he whispered.

Chapter Twenty-three
Saturday, June 23
4:48 p.m.

The man sitting in front of Molly wasn't what she had expected, having spent days literally envisioning his voice and temperament, seeing him as a killer. Bob Watson was polite, intelligent and soft spoken, and Molly now understood why Ari and Sol Gardner had proclaimed his innocence. What had begun as a formal interview had progressed into a pleasant conversation minus the scripted questions Molly had prepared, the chief and the district attorney having already assured Bob that he would not be arrested for any crime, since in the end he helped apprehend the killer and saved the life of a civilian. To take him into custody for his flight would be bad PR.

She was sure Ari had not told Bob about their relationship, but so far he had steered the conversation away from her every time Molly tried to bring it up, like two drivers fighting for control of the same car. After twenty minutes she gave up, unable to slake her thirst for knowledge of the real estate agent. She knew Ari was resting in the hospital and would make a full recovery, but she knew nothing else. When they had arrived at the house, Molly had jumped out of the car, only to watch the ambulance pull away at the same time. During the next few hours they tried to piece together what happened, culminating in the current interview she was having with Bob Watson.

"Of course, I knew that either Kristen or Lily was the killer," he was saying, "and my money was on Kristen."

"How did you know?" Molly automatically asked and clicked the end of her pen to take notes.

"She got a fax while I was there. I pulled it off the machine, and it said something about changing the meeting time to seven thirty. When Thorndike was dead the next day, I thought about that fax, and I thought about some of the little things that seemed off about Kristen."

"Off?" Molly asked.

Bob cracked his knuckles and reached for his chewing gum. "Yeah, it never seemed right between us." He shook his head. "Just little things," he added before stopping abruptly. "Let's just say I thought it was very convenient."

"Why didn't you just tell me this in the first place? Why did you run?"

He rubbed his hands together and stared at the floor. "It was complicated. After I drove away, I felt like an idiot for being so blinded by Kristen. I thought she loved me."

"So why did you suspect Lily?"

"I knew she'd started seeing him again, and I also knew that he wasn't going to leave his wife, even though he wanted to."

"Why not?"

Bob smiled. "Two words—community property." Bob looked down and blushed, very embarrassed. "You see, when I thought that I would leave Lily for Kristen, I wanted the best for Lily. I thought if she had someone, then maybe my leaving wouldn't be so bad. So I met with him." He shrugged his shoulders and glanced at Molly for her reaction.

Molly raised an eyebrow. "What did he say?"

"He said he was leaving his wife, but for some woman he'd met through work. They'd had a huge fight when he told her, but she was beginning to accept it." Bob wiped his face with his hand. "Little did I know his mistress was *my* mistress."

"Did he say anything about the bribe?"

"Not a word," Bob insisted. "You know, it was pretty funny. We actually buried the hatchet. The two of us spent fifteen minutes or so joking about divorce and alimony. He asked me about prenuptial agreements and if I had one with Lily. That was a hoot. When Lily and I met, we didn't have two nickels to rub together. That made me think about how much money Lily was going to get, but I didn't care. I told him, if he was smart he'd make his new wife sign on the dotted line before he said 'I do.' Then he gave me one of those knowing looks, and we shook hands. I still can't believe it, but I actually shook that poor bastard's hand.

"The thing is, Michael Thorndike loved money more than anything, and there was no way he would risk losing half his fortune. When he was killed, I suspected he had changed his mind, and his lover had shot him in a jealous rage after he told her. So I confronted Lily, but she told me the truth." Molly looked at him quizzically. "She didn't care about marrying him. They could just keep sleeping together." The pain in Bob's face was obvious, and Molly felt so sorry for a man who had been through a week of hell in many ways. "But he dumped her anyway for Kristen." He chewed furiously on the wad of gum and looked Molly straight in the eye. "When Lily left the motel, I knew she wasn't the killer. And I knew she really had loved Thorndike."

"I'm sorry," Molly said.

"It's okay," he shrugged. "I'm not so attached to my money. When I ask Lily for a divorce, it will be a relief in many ways." He shifted in the chair. "Back to the story. So, I thought the murderer was Kristen, but I had to be sure. So I called her and told her where I was, and darned if you people didn't show up on my doorstep the next day," he said sarcastically.

"So she was the anonymous tip, and you knew we were coming, so you got out," Molly concluded. "So where did you go next?"

Bob leaned back and smiled at the loaded question. "I'm taking the fifth on that one. But I did start following Kristen."

"Please tell me you didn't stay with Ari," Molly said quietly, looking Bob straight in the eye.

"No." Satisfied, Molly put her notebook away and prepared to leave. The room was heavy with Molly's obvious sadness.

"Have you spoken with her?" Bob asked casually.

She cleared her throat before answering. "No, and I don't anticipate needing to see her again."

Bob laughed heartily. "Come on, Detective. You're probably a good cop but you're not going to win an Oscar." Molly looked away, her emotions beginning to swirl. Bob leaned over and patted her knee. "Let me tell you a story, okay?" Still unable to look him in the face, Molly nodded.

"The day that Ari told her parents she was gay, her father disowned her and gave her twenty minutes to pack up and get out. When I got home from work, I found her in our apartment, sobbing in Lily's arms. We let her stay in the guest room, but Lily sensed that Ari was in deep trouble. Lily was a psychology major in college and she would have been a damn good shrink if she'd ever finished," he added. "Anyway, what you need to know about Ari, Detective, is that she's methodical, an incredible planner. The third night she was there, we went to bed, leaving her on the couch watching TV. I remember it was winter, and it was cold.

Ari was wrapped up in a blanket, her legs tucked underneath her. She looked so small and fragile."

He took a breath before he continued. "We said good night and went to bed. I stayed up reading for a while, but by eleven thirty, I was ready to fall asleep. I remember turning the light out and lying in the darkness, but I couldn't close my eyes. I felt something was wrong, like I'd forgotten to do something like lock the door. It was just a dumb feeling. Anyway, I tried to shrug it off, because I really was very tired, but it kept me awake. I got out of bed and went to check on Ari." He stopped and stared at Molly, his face solemn. "To this day, I can't tell you why I got up. I can't tell you why—I just knew something was wrong." Molly guessed what was coming. "She was unconscious, Lily's sleeping pills and my bottle of vodka on the bed." His voice cracked and he took Molly's hand. "She was so damn smart. She'd spent two days planning this, finding Lily's pills. The doctor said she took just the right amount." He gave a halfhearted laugh. "You know, Ari's not one to waste anything. If she could kill herself with ten, why take twenty? She almost died, she wanted to die. If I hadn't gotten up . . ." His voice trailed off and he closed his eyes. "She was only twenty-two."

Molly thought of Ari's words on her patio. "So she owed you," Molly summarized.

Bob shook his head. "It's never been about owing me anything. I'd do it again for her. I'd do anything for her. If she'd told me that I *had* to turn myself in, I would have done it."

"But she didn't," Molly said, both of them fully understanding her point.

Bob let it go and held up his hands for emphasis. "Here's the thing, Detective. You never stood a chance against me." Molly's face colored at Bob's superior attitude. "Ari has a tough time letting people get close. Everyone she's loved has abandoned her in one way or another—except me. Her track record with women sucks, and every time she breaks up, it's old Bob to comfort her. You never stood a chance."

"Lucky you," Molly snorted, making no attempt to hide her hurt.

"No, lucky you," Bob retorted. "Most of her girlfriends were losers, never knew what they had—especially her last one, Trina. That bitch was a golddigger who just wanted Ari's money. Did you know Ari's rich?"

"No, we never talked about it."

"She'll be a millionaire by the time she's forty, if she takes my advice," he said with a wink.

"Good for her," Molly replied, unimpressed.

"Doesn't sway you?" he asked, rising to leave.

Her eyes narrowed at the baiting comment. "It offends me. Money isn't an issue for me in relationships."

Bob's eyes twinkled. "Well, then I guess Ari's lucky that you're in love with her," he said, walking out the door before Molly could protest.

The hospital corridor reeked of ammonia and wet streaks lined the linoleum. Molly automatically gripped the vase tighter and checked the floor beneath her. The last thing she needed was to wind up in a hospital bed herself. The repeated ding of the elevator announced its descent. She turned to the information, desk, debating whether to just leave the flowers with a note. She was just about to chicken out when the doors opened and its passengers filed out around her.

"Well, well, Detective Nelson. Imagine meeting you here." Molly nearly dropped the flowers at the sight of Jane holding open the elevator door with her arm. "Going up?" Molly nodded absently, repositioning her hands around the vase. Jane stared at Molly, her finger perched on the "door open" button, her lips tightly shut. All Molly could do was join her in the moving prison. The doors closed and Jane hit the stop button. The elevator and Molly's stomach both lurched at the same time. Jane leaned back against the fake paneling, her arms folded across her chest.

"So is this a peace offering?" Jane asked, motioning to the flowers.

"I just wanted to see how she's doing," Molly said. Her eyes met Jane's, and she blinked. The woman's face was taut, her green eyes on fire.

"I hope you're planning on apologizing," Jane said frankly.

"For what?" Molly blurted. Although she was very worried about Ari, her pride wouldn't allow her to forget that Ari had lied to her.

Jane raised an eyebrow and her lips curved into a smug smile. "Ari's not the only one who's hidden something this week, has she, Detective?"

General bewilderment spread across Molly's face. "I don't know what you mean."

"I saw you at Hideaway with the redhead," Jane said.

Molly's chin dropped to her chest, and she caught a strong whiff of the blooming lilies. "I guess she won't see me then, will she?" she whispered. Her eyes filled with tears, and she stared at the flowers.

"I didn't tell her."

Jane watched Molly's crestfallen face register the fact. "I'm not one to judge. I was there, too, and I certainly didn't sleep in my own bed that night." Molly's arms tightened around the vase and she closed her eyes. Jane stepped toward her and stroked one of the lily petals with her lacquered nails. "You and I aren't like Ari." Molly looked at Jane, realizing how right she was. "Have you been tested?" Jane asked.

"Yes, recently," Molly nodded adamantly.

The muscles of Jane's face relaxed slightly. "Good. The idea of Ari contracting anything . . ." She stepped back and pressed the elevator button, both of them listening as the elevator strained to ascend again. The doors opened at the eighth floor, and Molly hesitated, wanting to thank Jane, but not knowing how. She stepped out of the elevator and turned around.

"If you want her back, you had better not do anything to make her unhappy." The tone in Jane's voice was unmistakably deadly. Although Molly was almost a foot taller and could have cast a shadow over Jane's entire body, she was intimidated by the slight woman whose loyalty was unwavering. Molly stood there mute for a full minute after the doors had closed on Jane's words.

She found Ari's room and held her breath as she walked through the doorway. Relief and disappointment overtook her at the sight of the beautiful woman sleeping. She set the vase on the nightstand, careful not to make a noise, and turned to the bed. The sight of Ari's bandage protruding from her hospital gown brought tears to Molly's eyes, and she instinctively stroked her hair in comfort. Standing there, her heart pounding in her chest, she knew Bob's last words to her were true, but it would be a long time before she admitted her feelings to Ari or anyone else. She leaned over and kissed Ari's forehead gently.

Soft footsteps crossed the tile, but Ari couldn't open her eyes. Maybe it was a dream. The medications were working—she couldn't focus, but she could smell the musk that hovered in the air. Molly. As the footsteps retreated toward the door, Ari opened her eyes in time to see Molly depart, her head down and her shoulders hunched. She looked beaten down, and a wave of sympathy swept through Ari. She opened her mouth to call out, but Molly was gone. Or was it a dream?

Noises from the hall drew Ari's attention to the doorway. Two children scampered past, their laughter prompting a sharp reprimand from an elderly woman who hurried by after them. A young couple trailed behind, armed with balloons and flowers.

The woman glanced into Ari's room, her face already molded into a sympathetic expression. It was the same face Ari wore whenever she walked into a hospital. The suffering was all around, amidst the white gowns, IV drips and beeping machines.

Ari had never been hospitalized before, not even as a child. How she managed to avoid breaking a bone, needing stitches or even cracking open her skull, amazed her parents. In fact, Ari had never crossed a hospital's threshold until three days after her twelfth birthday—the day her mother entered the hospital for chemotherapy and her first of three bouts with cancer. Hospital visits became routine, and her mother's illness remained the most vivid memory of her teenage years. When the cancer finally took her mother's life, Ari avoided hospitals, and she had never again been inside one except for the unexpected visit to the emergency room following her attempted suicide. Even then, she refused to be admitted.

The drugs were definitely working, numbing the pain in Ari's shoulder. Thanks to Bob's quick actions, she'd been in surgery within thirty minutes of being shot, and she would make a full recovery. She closed her eyes to shut out the last few hours, the confrontation with Kristen, the pain, Jane's worried face, an empty hospital room.

A long time ago Ari had made a deal with herself on the advice of a therapist. She could think of her mother for twenty minutes a day, but no more. To dwell on the past would send her into a deep depression—of this she was sure. She'd been there before. Usually if she thought of other things, her mother's image would fade, a fact that gave Ari relief and shame at the same time. Today, though, the other thoughts were too horrible, and her mother, and surprisingly, her father, filled her mind. Maybe it was the meds. Maybe it was the hospital. Maybe it was shock. Maybe it was because she was totally alone.

Ari's gaze shifted to the nightstand and the beautiful arrangement of lilies. Tears streamed down her cheeks and it befuddled her. In the last two hours she'd faced a murderer, been saved by her best friend, and in her mind, abandoned again by her family. Yet, a vase full of flowers made her cry. She couldn't understand it. A tiny white envelope protruded amongst the lilies. Ari plucked the card from the plastic holder and stared at the short message:

I'm sorry. Can we forget the last week and try again?

Ari smiled. Suddenly she didn't feel so alone. She closed her eyes, breathing in the scent of Molly's cologne and thinking about the future. When the phone rang, it was tempting to ignore it. The medications were really taking hold and Ari was ready for sleep again. Still, she found herself reaching for the receiver out of habit.

"Hello?"

The voice on the other end was immediately recognizable, although she could barely understand what he said, the poor connection and his distress garbling his words. When he finally took a breath from his harangue, Ari paused and smiled before she spoke.

"I'm okay, Dad."